'You did a [...] Amanda.'

'So did you,' she returned shyly. Then she smiled wryly. 'Not the best re-introduction to Ashburton for you.'

'Oh, I don't know,' Jack said thoughtfully. 'In some ways it's made me feel like I've really arrived. I've felt like a tourist until now.'

Amanda nodded. 'There's a big difference,' she agreed.

Did she mean a big difference for him? Or for herself in her opinion of him? He realised he had completely forgotten their acrimonious exchange that morning.

'I'm sorry about this morning,' he told her slowly. 'I guess I was still a tourist.' He watched her closely, wondering whether she understood.

This time Amanda smiled as she nodded. 'Apology accepted from Mr Armstrong.' She raised her wine glass in a toast. 'Welcome to Ashburton, Jack.'

Alison Roberts was born in New Zealand, and says, 'I lived in London and Washington D.C. as a child and began my working career as a primary-school teacher. A lifelong interest in medicine was fostered by my doctor and nurse parents, flatting with doctors and physiotherapists on leaving home and marriage to a house surgeon who is now a consultant cardiologist. I have also worked as a cardiology technician and research assistant. My husband's medical career took us to Glasgow for two years, which was an ideal place and time to start my writing career. I now live in Christchurch, New Zealand with my husband, daughter and various pets.'

Recent titles by the same author:

MORE THAN A MISTRESS
ONE OF A KIND
MUM'S THE WORD
A CHANCE IN A MILLION

PERFECT TIMING

BY
ALISON ROBERTS

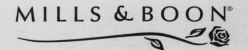

MILLS & BOON®

All the characters in this book have no existence outside the imagination of the author, and have no relation whatsoever to anyone bearing the same name or names. They are not even distantly inspired by any individual known or unknown to the author, and all the incidents are pure invention.

First published in Great Britain 1999
Harlequin Mills & Boon Limited,
Eton House, 18-24 Paradise Road, Richmond, Surrey TW9 1SR

© Alison Roberts 1999

ISBN 0 263 81893 4

Set in Times Roman 10½ on 12 pt.
03-9912-45386-D

Printed and bound in Spain
by Litografia Rosés S.A., Barcelona

CHAPTER ONE

THE noise emitted from the paging device was demanding.

Jack Armstrong snorted incredulously. He was still shaking his head as he pulled his car to a smooth halt in the assigned parking slot of Ashburton General Hospital's consultant surgeon.

It wasn't so much that the range of the pager extended as far as the car park that amazed him. It wasn't that it was only 7.45 a.m. and he wasn't officially on duty until 8 a.m. It was more the fact that Ashburton General had pagers at all.

'Ashburton *General*,' he muttered, reaching over to collect his briefcase and the now innocently silent pager. 'Ashburton *only*, more like.'

Jack Armstrong eased his long frame from the car and slammed the door shut. His discontented gaze raked the old wooden building with its gables and verandahs and the large covered porch that announced the main entrance. It didn't look any larger than the house he had just left. Why on earth did they even bother with pagers? They could just lean out of a window or over a bannister and call someone.

Jack failed to notice the cheerful greeting and wave from the elderly man tending the garden. He was in no mood to respond even if he had. This was a mistake, he was sure of it. He had had his misgivings even as he'd agreed to do the locum yesterday. The hospital administrator had been younger than his own mere thirty-six years. Young and enthusiastic. You would have thought that the position of managing the only medical establishment in a one-horse town was the pinnacle of his career. Jack had made it clear that he was doing them an enormous favour and the administrator, Kevin Farrow, had been suitably appreciative.

'It's an incredible stroke of luck,' he had told Jack delightedly. 'Not only are you a general surgeon but you've had extensive obstetric experience. You're a godsend.'

'Only a temporary one,' Jack had reminded him curtly.

'Three months should be plenty of time for us to attract a suitable replacement.' Kevin Farrow sounded confident.

Jack had raised one eyebrow. 'Really?'

Kevin had only looked momentarily disconcerted by the dubious tone. He cleared his throat and grinned. 'Let me show you around and introduce you. It shouldn't take long.'

'I'm sure it wouldn't,' Jack agreed with a small smile. 'But I'm afraid I must decline. I expect I'll meet everyone soon enough when I come on duty tomorrow.'

'Of course. You must have a lot to consider with your family commitments. I don't suppose you've even got over the jet lag yet.'

Jet lag had been the least of his worries. And he was over it quite well enough to realise that he wouldn't be able to stand being cooped up in that mausoleum of a house with his father without some means of distraction. The locum position at the hospital had seemed a godsend to him as well when he'd read of it in the newspaper. But now he wasn't so sure.

Jack Armstrong's powerful legs took the short flight of steps to the porch in two strides. He stood in front of the main doors for a second, before remembering that they didn't open automatically. Irritated, he gave the large door a firm shove and stepped inside. He felt trapped. He had probably only added another unwelcome dimension to his visit by taking on this locum and with his luck he would probably be stuck here for the whole three months of his arranged leave of absence.

His father would undoubtedly take pleasure in making sure he stayed alive that long. To enjoy his obvious ill health. Or, rather, to enjoy denying the fact that he was dying and to refuse to allow his only son to even discuss it, let alone offer any medical assistance. The housekeeper had been convinced it was only a matter of weeks.

The letter had come as a shock even after almost twenty years of no contact. Enough of a shock to make Jack ponder the regret that might ensue if he made no effort to come to terms with the past. Enough of a shock to make him arrange a leave of absence from a position he was more than happy with and travel to a God-forsaken village on the other side of the world. After more than ten years in London he couldn't believe how dead Ashburton seemed.

Small country, small town, small hospital. Jack did notice the hospital receptionist but only nodded at her effusively welcoming greeting. His attention had been caught by the large white board beside her desk.

'83 days to go,' the board announced importantly. 'Ashburton General welcomes the new millennium.'

Jack wondered how long the board had been counting off the days. It had probably been the most exciting topic of conversation around here for the last decade. Or perhaps the board usually informed people of how many shopping days there were before Christmas. He sighed heavily. Small people, small minds. Millennium fever had gripped the world, of course. The event was being exploited for an infinite variety of commercial advertising or worthy causes but it was overwhelming on this side of the globe. New Zealand would be the first nation to greet the new millennium and the local pride in this fact of nature was pathetic.

He had read recently that the last time around Armageddon had been expected and had provoked all manner of strange behaviour amongst people. One might have expected things to have improved a little more with a thousand years of collective experience.

Jack Armstrong's moody perusal of the board was interrupted as his pager sounded again. The receptionist, whose name he hadn't bothered registering, looked up brightly.

'There's a phone here you can use, Mr Armstrong.' She pushed it helpfully across the desk.

Jack grunted and picked up the receiver. He listened to the dial tone.

'Ring "O",' the girl told him with a smile. 'That's "O" for operator. See? That's Marcia over there.' She pointed to a cubicle at the end of the reception desk. Another young girl with an earphones and microphone headset grinned and waved through the glass panel of the door. 'Marcia will connect you.'

Jack pushed the appropriate button. He wouldn't have been surprised if Marcia had been sitting in front of a telephone that needed to have a handle wound.

'Hello, Mr Armstrong. Welcome to Ashburton General,' Marcia chirped.

'Yes,' Jack agreed. It was understandable that he was so welcome. He was, after all, a godsend. He just wasn't sure he could reciprocate the enthusiasm. Jack broke the slightly awkward silence that had fallen. 'You have a call for me, Mary?'

'Marcia. Yes, Amanda Morrison is on the line. I'll put you through now.'

Who the hell was Amanda Morrison? Maybe he should have gritted his teeth and done the grand tour with young Kevin Farrow yesterday.

'Hello, Mr Armstrong.'

'That's correct.'

'I'm Amanda Morrison. Welcome to Ashburton. I hope you'll enjoy your visit with us.'

'I hope so, too.' Jack's tone didn't suggest it was likely. He sighed. There would probably be a cake for morning tea with a welcoming message piped on in icing. 'What can I do for you, Dr Morrison?'

'Not doctor. I'm a nurse,' Amanda informed him. 'I'm in the obstetric unit. I have a fifteen-year-old primigravida who's—'

'*How* old?'

'Fifteen.'

'Good God. Don't you teach children about contraception in this neck of the woods?'

The stunned silence at the other end of the line gave Jack time to register the expression of the receptionist. He yanked the phone away to the full extent of its cable length and turned his back to the girl. The voice had returned on the phone line, sounding a lot less confident.

'I don't really think that's important, Mr Armstrong.'

'Really?' Jack felt the smallness of his surroundings closing in on him. Another example of small-town isolation and ignorance. 'Well, if that's the general attitude, no wonder you've got children having children.'

'I meant at this particular moment.' The voice now sounded confident again. But not friendly. 'I have a patient with a posterior presentation who's been in labour for nearly fourteen hours. She's fully dilated but tiring and is in considerable pain. I would like you to see her with a view to a possible epidural and acceleration.'

'Do you have an anaesthetist available?'

'Of course.' The voice was very close to a snap. 'I doubt that we'd be employing a locum surgeon without having one available.'

'I meant at this particular moment.' Jack almost smiled. He was suddenly aware that this antagonistic exchange was rather a good distraction from his previous mood. Quite enjoyable, in fact. 'This isn't exactly a huge institution,' he continued. 'Who is the anaesthetist?'

'Tom Kearney. Would you like me to contact him?'

'No. I'll see the patient myself first, thank you. I'll be there as soon as I find out where you are.'

'That shouldn't be too difficult.' The tone was clipped and very cool. 'As you say, we're not a huge institution.'

Amanda Morrison stared at the phone for a few seconds, having replaced the receiver without waiting for a reply. What a nerve! Kevin Farrow had sounded so enthusiastic about the locum appointment when he'd talked to Amanda yesterday. Did he have any idea that Mr Armstrong considered them to be uneducated country bumpkins who were practising medicine in the equivalent of a tin shack? Shaking the mop of black curls that framed a normally very cheerful face, Amanda grimaced at the young woman standing nearby, holding a stack of clean linen.

'What did he say?'

'That we should be handing out contraceptive advice.'

'Bit late for that.'

Amanda nodded. 'Exactly.' She looked at her companion with concern. 'You look totally exhausted, Libby. How long have you been on duty?'

'Young Chloe Worbeton came in at six o'clock last night,' Libby replied wearily. 'And then Helen Page came in an hour ago.'

'Helen's in again?' Amanda grinned. 'How many is it now?'

'It's her fifth. She's doing fine. I expect she could deliver it herself. It's Chloe I'm worried about. I was staying to talk it over with Grace but when she rang to say she had the flu I thought I'd better call you.'

'I'm glad you did,' Amanda said, nodding. 'Can you manage Helen for the moment?'

'Of course.' Libby smiled. 'We probably won't get another delivery for a week after this. Never rains but it pours.'

Amanda returned the midwife's smile. 'Let's hope not. You look like you could use a good rest. We don't want you coming down with this nasty flu. At least we've got a surgeon available now so we won't have to ship Chloe off to Christchurch.'

'We don't often get a new man around here.' Libby wriggled her eyebrows at Amanda, before moving towards the door of Room 1. 'I'm looking forward to meeting him.'

'I'm not sure I am,' Amanda murmured. She took a deep breath, crossed the corridor and pushed open the door of Room 2.

The girl looked much younger than her fifteen years. Perhaps Mr Armstrong might have more sympathy when he actually met Chloe Worbeton. Any sophistication or confidence the teenager might normally possess had been eroded by the fear her present situation was causing. White-faced, she clung to her mother's hand. A child again, seeking reassurance and prepared to abdicate any decisions that needed to be made. Amanda recognised the fear only too well. It didn't seem to make any difference how many years went by. Obstetrics was always a difficult area to work in and a teenage delivery especially hard to handle.

Amanda squeezed the girl's hand, before reaching for her pulse. 'You're doing really well, Chloe. It shouldn't be too much longer.'

Chloe nodded wearily.

'It makes it a lot more difficult to cope with the pain when you're tired, doesn't it?'

Chloe nodded again. Amanda could see that tears were not far away. Amanda held out the most recent section of trace paper released by the foetal monitor beside the bed. The present heart rate was 127 and steady. The baby was in less distress than its mother. The graph became more erratic as a new contraction started. Chloe groaned loudly and then cried out, turning her face into the pillow. Her mother looked across at Amanda.

'Can't we do something to speed things up, Nurse? All we want is to get this over with and put it all behind us. It seems to be taking far too long.'

'I've called the consultant,' Amanda told her. 'I imagine he'll want to arrange some pain relief for Chloe and then—'

'Oh, we don't want anything that's going to slow things down,' Brenda Worbeton interrupted. 'Like we told the midwife and the registrar that came a while back. Chloe can cope. She's very—'

'I think we all want what's best for Chloe.' Amanda's interruption was firm. 'And for the baby. Let's wait and see what he says.'

'Is that Mr Brogan, then?' Brenda Worbeton rubbed her hand over her forehead and sighed heavily. 'He delivered Chloe, you know.'

'No. Hadn't you heard? Mr Brogan had a heart attack a couple of months ago and has retired early. We've just got a locum in fortunately. A general surgeon but with plenty of experience in obstetrics.'

Brenda frowned. 'I was expecting Mr Brogan

would be here if anything went wrong. Is this new chap any good?'

'I'm sure he is.' Amanda smiled confidently at Chloe who was managing to look even more fearful at the turn of conversation. She suppressed the thought that his professional skills had better outweigh his charm or they would all be in trouble. 'I haven't actually met him myself yet,' she confessed to Brenda. 'He's been working in London hospitals for the last ten years and he has excellent references. His name's Jack Armstrong.'

'I went to school with a Jack Armstrong.' Brenda sounded surprised. 'I wonder if it's him?'

'I doubt it.' Amanda was about to voice the thought that Jack Armstrong didn't sound like someone who had ever had, or wanted to have, any association with a small town when the door opened behind her.

So this was the sophisticated Londonite who had deigned to rescue Ashburton General from its surgical desert. The dark, three-piece, pin-striped suit looked like a Harley Street necessity. Amanda's eyes widened. A waistcoat of all things! He was going to look as out of place here as a bottle of champagne in a crate of beer. Her gaze flicked up but only caught a profile as Jack Armstrong nodded towards her patient and reached for the clipboard attached to the end of Chloe's bed.

Straight hair, almost as dark as her own. Cut short at the back but with enough length on top to make a section flop over his forehead as he bent his head to read the chart. Elegantly straight nose and a mouth twisted into a very professionally thoughtful line.

Brenda Worbeton was staring as hard as Amanda

at the newcomer. It took her only seconds to break the silence.

'It *is* you!' she exclaimed. 'Jack Armstrong!'

The flop of hair was returned to its rightful place by only a mild jerk of his head as the surgeon transferred his gaze. 'That's correct.' The tone was cool. 'And you are Chloe's mother?'

'I'm Brenda. Brenda Worbeton.' The wide grin faded as she waited for an expected reaction that didn't arrive. 'I suppose it *was* a long time ago.' She gave him another chance. 'Arthur Street primary school? It was you, wasn't it?'

'I did attend the school.' Jack's gaze left Brenda and slid suddenly towards Amanda. 'As you say, it was a long time ago.' He extended his hand. 'Jack Armstrong,' he said unnecessarily.

'Amanda Morrison.' Amanda held the direct look from a pair of dark blue eyes. She took the hand and found her own squeezed in a brief but very firm greeting.

Brenda was still staring at him. 'You must remember, surely? We sat together in standard two. It was you who put the mouse in Mrs Allen's lunchbox.'

The groan from Chloe was delayed just long enough for Amanda to register the fact that Jack was ignoring Brenda.

'I'll have some gloves, thank you, Nurse. Mrs Worbeton, perhaps you could wait outside while I examine Chloe.'

The examination was thorough but Amanda refused to be impressed. He's competent, she conceded to herself, and she couldn't complain about his treatment of Chloe. He had explained his examination and findings carefully and had refrained from any inappropriate remarks about contraception. His interaction with both herself and Brenda, however, gave quite a lot of scope for complaint. Jack Armstrong was unfriendly, patronising and just plain rude.

'Right.' Jack pulled his jacket off the hook behind the door. He spoke quietly to Amanda. 'It's beyond me why you didn't go for a full epidural when she first came in. You must have known that an occiputo posterior presentation would be likely to produce a long labour and severe back pain. She hasn't even had any morphine, for heaven's sake.'

'That was Chloe's choice,' Amanda returned coolly. 'But I agree. Had I been involved in the case earlier I would certainly have advised more pain control.'

'Too late now.' Jack Armstrong eased the fit of his jacket. 'Move Chloe to the delivery room. You'll have to use gas.' He raised his voice. 'Don't forget, Chloe. It's time for a bit of hard work for you. It's called labour for a very good reason.' He reached for the doorhandle and nodded at Amanda. 'See what you can do. Give me a call in an hour if there's still no progress.'

'Let's sit you up a bit further, Chloe. It might put some pressure on your baby's head and move it more easily.' Amanda supported Chloe with one arm and rearranged the pillows. 'Take a deep breath when the pain comes and push down. Put your chin on your chest and imagine pushing right down through the centre of your body. Mum will help you hold on the gas mask when you inhale.' Amanda glanced at her watch. The hour was almost up. She would give it one more contraction before examining Chloe again. 'No grunting,' she reminded the tired teenager gently. 'It makes the push less effective.' The running commentary Amanda was giving by way of encouragement was automatic. 'Good girl. Breathe out while you push. Keep pushing. Take another breath. Push, push, push! You're doing really well, Chloe. Take another breath. It's the third push that does the most work.'

When Libby came in a few minutes later with a glass of chipped ice for Chloe, Amanda took the opportunity to slip out of the room with her briefly.

'How's Helen?'

'All done. Another boy. She's ready to go home, she says.'

'That's where you should be going.'

'How's Chloe doing?'

'No progress and she's in too much pain. I'm just going to call Mr Armstrong again.'

'What's he like?'

'Too sophisticated for the likes of us, Libby. But he seems to know what he's doing.'

The impression of Mr Armstrong's competence was consolidated over the next thirty minutes. He arrived in the company of Tom Kearney, the anaesthetist, and Amanda was kept busy assisting them both. Chloe was given a short-acting epidural which took the edge off her pain but allowed her to continue pushing. The contractions were now getting further apart and weakening, however, so an oxytocin infusion was started. Amanda kept an eye on the foetal monitor.

'Heart rate's increasing. Up to 150,' she reported after the next contraction.

Chloe was crying. 'I can't push any more,' she sobbed. 'I'm too tired.'

Brenda looked as exhausted as her daughter. 'You're doing well, love. Don't give up now. It'll all be over soon.'

Jack Armstrong caught Amanda's glance and he nodded. 'I think we'll get this baby out for you now, Chloe.' He moved towards the basin and reached for a scrubbing brush. 'I'm going to help it out with some forceps, OK?'

Chloe nodded and reached for her mother's hand. Brenda also nodded gratefully.

'I'm going to put your feet up into these stirrups, Chloe,' Amanda advised. 'When Mr Armstrong tells you, you'll need to push and he'll pull at the same time.'

'Will it hurt?' Chloe's voice was a whisper.

Amanda draped sterile linen over Chloe's legs and reached for a bowl of antiseptic and a swab. 'You'll feel a dragging sensation as the baby is delivered, which is uncomfortable but it shouldn't be painful.'

'We'll do an episiotomy first,' Jack added. 'I'm just putting in some local anaesthetic now. Scissors, thanks, Nurse.'

Amanda had the forceps ready as well and the suction equipment which she used only minutes later to clear out the baby girl's airways. The baby opened its mouth and gave a tentative wail. Jack nodded as he reached for a clamp.

'One minute Apgar of 8.' He cut the cord and picked up the baby to lay it on the clean towel Amanda was holding out. 'You can get her to the nursery and do the five-minute Apgar score there, if you like.'

Amanda's mouth dropped open. 'Our babies always stay with their mothers,' she said in astonishment.

'Not in this case, surely?'

Amanda lowered her voice. 'Why should this case be any different?'

Jack Armstrong raised an eyebrow. 'I understood the baby was being given up for adoption.'

'So?' Amanda's voice was a hiss. 'Does that make it acceptable for the mother not to have a chance to bond with the child?'

'It's debatable.'

'Possibly.' Amanda fixed Jack with an icy glare. 'But this is neither an appropriate time nor place for such a debate.' She finished wiping the baby's face with damp gauze. The infant's cries which had masked the brief but heated exchange now abruptly stopped. Amanda turned her back on Jack.

'You have a beautiful little girl, Chloe. Would you like to hold her?'

Kevin Farrow was waving at Amanda excitedly. 'I've just had a phone call from Television New Zealand,' he told her as soon as she moved within earshot.

'Don't tell me!' The characteristic dimples in Amanda's cheeks appeared as she smiled broadly. 'Our new locum is actually an international superstar and the media have just discovered the quaint country town he's hiding in.'

Kevin returned the smile. 'He's certainly dressed for the part, isn't he?'

Amanda eyed Kevin's open-necked shirt and baggy trousers. Kevin was trendy, always tidy but never overly formal. He fitted in just fine. His recent engagement to Linda, one of the theatre nurses, had further consolidated his position as one of the team.

'At least he knows what he's doing,' Amanda conceded. 'We had a difficult delivery this morning and he handled a set of forceps more than adequately.'

'That's good to hear.' Kevin sounded suddenly serious. 'References can only go so far to tell you what you really need to know.'

'Mmm. They never mention attitude, do they?'

'Is there a problem?'

Amanda shook her head. 'I wouldn't say that. I just got the impression he's not that happy to be here.'

'I'm not surprised. The reason he came here is because his father's dying, apparently.'

'Oh, I didn't know,' Amanda said sympathetically. She frowned slightly. A family crisis might excuse quite a lot of attitude but it didn't seem like the sole explanation for Jack Armstrong's behaviour. Still, perhaps she should give her opinion of the man a second chance. 'What were you going to tell me, Kevin?'

Kevin Farrow's eyes brightened. 'Did you know Dorothy McFadden is due to turn one hundred?'

Amanda nodded. Dorothy was one of their select group of long-stay geriatric patients. 'She's looking forward to her telegram from the queen.'

'Do you know when her birthday is?'

This time Amanda shook her head. 'Not exactly. I've been meaning to look it up. Some time early in the year, I think.'

'Very early.' Kevin was almost bursting with excitement. 'January the first early.'

'New Year's Day?'

'New Century's Day. New Millennium's Day. Do you have any idea what this means?'

'Um. An extra party?' Amanda sighed inwardly. The hype for the new millennium was almost becoming an irritation. People were coming to see it as a new beginning—a start of a wonderful new era. It was a remarkable event, certainly, but it wasn't going to change anyone's life.

'A huge party,' Kevin breathed. 'And we're going to be issuing the invitations.'

'I don't think Dorothy will want a big fuss,' Amanda cautioned. 'She's hanging on to her dignity with enormous determination.'

Kevin took a big breath. 'Dorothy McFadden is the only person in New Zealand to be turning one hundred on New Year's Day. Hell, she's probably the only person in the southern hemisphere! That means she will be the first person in the *world* to turn one hundred in the new millennium.' He lowered his voice importantly. 'The media are interested. Very interested. If they are interested in Dorothy McFadden they will also be interested in Ashburton General.' He put a hand on both Amanda's shoulders and gave an excited squeeze. 'This is a PR dream. It'll put us on the map. It could be the only thing standing between us and closure.'

Amanda sighed audibly this time. The threat of the hospital's closure, or at least considerable downgrading, was real enough. Ashburton was under an hour's drive from the major tertiary centre of Christchurch. Government policy was rapidly whittling down rural services. It had been quite a victory to be allowed to replace their surgeon and keep their surgical services viable.

Kevin Farrow had made it his mission to try and save the entire hospital. The town supported him—demanded it, in fact—and Amanda supported him. Of course she did. She had no desire to work in a big city hospital even if she could still live in a rural area and commute with reasonable ease. Her job here was unique. It was her life and she loved it. Kevin had come up with many schemes to fight bureaucracy on behalf of the small hospital but Amanda had reservations about this particular inspiration.

'Strictly speaking, we should be discharging Dorothy into residential care or her own home,' Amanda said. 'It was only a very mild stroke that brought her in and we've got her heart failure and her diabetes under pretty good control now. She's remarkably well for her age.'

'But she doesn't have a home to go to,' Kevin said, horrified. 'She's certainly not well enough to travel back to Britain. And she doesn't know anybody in the town except us.'

'Yes. That's partly why we've kept her this long already,' Amanda agreed. 'And that nasty diabetic ulcer she's got on her foot has needed immobilisation. If it doesn't start improving I guess we could think about a skin graft—now that we have a surgeon available.'

'Excellent idea,' Kevin said with relief. 'Give it plenty of time to come right, though. We wouldn't want her to have a fall, trying to walk on it too soon.'

Amanda smiled reluctantly. 'Even so, I'm not sure Dorothy will be very happy about this idea. She's a very private person.'

'That's why I want you to talk to her about it.' Kevin's tone was persuasive. 'You know her better than anyone. You spend time with her every day.'

'I really like her.' Amanda smiled fondly. 'She reminds me of my grandmother.'

Kevin nodded happily. 'Everybody will like her. She'll be a celebrity. Local, national—international! And the vital, caring environment of the rural hospital she's in will be right there with her. I've already discussed that angle with the producer. She's keen. Might even do a separate documentary on us.'

'The media can be very intrusive. I'm not sure about this, Kevin.'

'Oh, come *on*, Mandy! This could be the only way to save the hospital. Surely it's worth tripping over a few cables for a while.' Kevin sounded desperate. *'Please!'*

Amanda had to laugh at the overdone expression. 'I'll talk to Dorothy,' she promised. 'I'm on my way to have lunch with her now. But if she's against the idea it'll be my responsibility to protect her.'

'Of course.' Kevin's face relaxed. 'I know you can do it, Amanda. I'm counting on you.'

Amanda balanced the tray carefully as she walked through the upstairs medical ward.

'Hi, Sandra. How's it going?'

The young nurse looked up from serving the patient lunches. 'Good, thanks, Mandy. Dorothy's out on the verandah.'

Amanda greeted each patient by name as she passed. There were only ten in this ward at present. The last was Mr Cooper. A retired sheep farmer, well into his eighties, Jim Cooper was another long-stay geriatric patient. Quite senile, Jim kept his hat on permanently and had to be watched carefully after 4 p.m. every day as he was convinced that he had to go out to attend to his dogs. Querulous and difficult at times, Amanda was pleased to see him sitting quietly, staring out the window at the distant rural scene.

'How are you, Mr Cooper?' she called cheerfully.

'Busy.' The tone was dismissive. 'Lambing season's always busy. Looks like rain, too.'

Amanda smiled. She could see the clear blue sky and knew that Dorothy would be in her favourite chair on the verandah, her tapestry work on her lap, enjoying the warmth of the spring sunshine. She set the tray down on a small table.

'Mrs Golder's done well again,' she told the elderly lady. 'Mashed egg and parsley sandwiches, soft bread and no crusts.' She picked up the teapot. 'The tea will be nice and strong by now, too. And, look, she's even put a rose on the tray for you.'

'She spoils me.' Dorothy McFadden's voice was surprisingly strong for her frail-looking body. 'And so do you, dear. You don't need to have lunch with me so often. You should spend your time with young people.'

'I like spending time with you,' Amanda responded. She moved the table closer so that Dorothy could reach her plate. 'Besides, I need to come up every day. I get a great view from here right into my back yard so I can check that Ralph is OK. I can see him now, lying in the sun and having a~go at his bone.'

'You're very fond of that dog.' Dorothy's cup rattled as she replaced it shakily.

'My gran gave him to me when I was having a bad spell. He's nearly eleven now and slowing down a bit.' Her voice softened. 'He's a very special friend.'

'I can't see that far,' Dorothy stated. 'I'm lucky to be able to see far enough to do my needlework now. What's your house like?'

'It's just a small flat,' Amanda told her. 'Joined to some others. My neighbours are all pensioners. It was my gran's house. She left it to me when she died. It's so convenient now I've never thought of shifting.'

Dorothy shook her head. She watched as Amanda picked up her own plate of whole-grain sandwiches. 'It doesn't do to become too settled,' she told her. 'Especially not at your age. You've got to be prepared to try new things. Risk a little adventure.'

'I'm quite happy,' Amanda said firmly. 'But if you have any desire for new adventures I've got something I promised Kevin Farrow I'd talk to you about.'

Dorothy's faded blue eyes focused on the young nurse.

'You can always say no,' Amanda added hurriedly. 'You're already special as far as we're concerned.' She took a sip from her cup of tea. 'It's just that your birthday and your age, with all this fuss about the new millennium, have attracted the attention of some television people. They would like to do a story about you.'

'A story? About me?' Dorothy looked confused. 'Who would see it?'

'A lot of people,' Amanda explained. 'And it would mean a lot of people coming to see you. With cameras and questions. It would be very tiring.'

'Would everybody see it? Everybody in Ashburton?'

'I expect so.' Amanda smiled. 'You'd be famous, Dorothy. I'm sure the whole town would be very excited about it.'

'Does he have a television?'

'Does who have a television?'

Dorothy McFadden stared blankly at Amanda who looked back with concern. Moments of confusion were only to be expected but it heightened her worry that this development would be too much for Dorothy. But the old woman's eyes suddenly focused again.

'Yes,' she said thoughtfully. Then more decisively, 'Yes. I think I'd like that, dear.'

'Are you sure? You might like some time to think about it.'

Amanda was treated to one of Dorothy McFadden's rare smiles. 'I don't need time to think, dear. It's like a frame, don't you see?'

Amanda shook her head.

'A story about me. It's like a frame around the picture my life has made and he...and people will see it. Even if they don't know the truth they will still see the picture.'

Amanda nodded but didn't understand. She thought

Dorothy's mind was wandering again. A hand, gnarled by rheumatism, moved to touch her own smooth skin.

'Something new, Amanda. It's an opportunity to start again. Or to complete something that needs finishing.' Dorothy leaned back in her armchair and closed her eyes. 'I didn't think I'd be lucky enough to get the chance again. Life is full of surprises.'

CHAPTER TWO

LIFE certainly was full of surprises.

Unfortunately, they were not all pleasant ones. Like the late season influenza virus that was doing the rounds of the staff at Ashburton General and playing havoc with staff rostering. Rostering that Amanda Morrison was responsible for.

Officially, that was the major component of Amanda's job. Ashburton General had three main wards. One was medical, one was for surgical and paediatric patients and one for assessment and rehabilitation with some long-term care for geriatric patients. Smaller units dealt with acute admissions, intensive care, obstetrics and day-surgery patients that needed to stay overnight. Amanda was responsible for the overall running of the wards and the rostering and recruitment of the nursing staff. Administrative paperwork was often relegated to after hours, however, as Amanda's real job satisfaction came from taking advantage of her considerable nursing experience and skills.

In the last eight years Amanda had worked in every area of the hospital. She was as confident assisting in Theatre or the emergency department as she was nursing in the geriatric or obstetric wards. Whatever specialist opportunity had presented itself over the years, Amanda had taken full advantage of it. She still studied voraciously and attended any training courses available, quite happy to allow the career she loved to consume almost every waking hour.

Now she could take delight in her wealth of experience and knowledge. Amanda made a point of trying to familiarise herself with every patient admitted to Ashburton General. She often knew every patient's name, relevant past history and the treatment they were undergoing. Amanda also acted as troubleshooter for staffing requirements, filling in whenever staffing absences or caseload pressure led to problems. It was Nurse Morrison who could always be called on in the middle of the night to assist with emergency surgery and it was Amanda who could help serve all the inpatient meals if Mrs Golder's bunions were proving particularly troublesome.

Well known, and immensely popular, Amanda Morrison was the lynchpin of both nursing and administrative staff and she was proud of her position and responsibilities.

Amanda hurried past the reception desk. The receptionist, Karen, had wiped off the large '83' on the whiteboard and was replacing it with a carefully drawn '82'. Amanda slowed her pace.

'You must be getting sick of that, Karen,' she commented. 'You've been doing it for ever!'

'Only since last New Year's Day,' Karen responded cheerfully. 'It's getting exciting now. Will you be going to the street party on New Year's Eve?'

'No, I'll be working.'

'As usual.' Karen shook her head. 'I suppose you'll be working Christmas again as well?'

'Somebody has to.'

'It doesn't always have to be you.'

Amanda smiled. It may as well be, she thought. What else did she have in her life? She kept the thought to herself, however. It would sound like a complaint if she voiced it and it wasn't. Amanda Morrison was quite happy with her life. It was exactly what she wanted. Well, almost exactly. She checked her watch.

'I'm going up to Theatre for the morning. Linda's off with this flu. Tell Marcia to take messages for me. If there are any urgent calls come up and catch me between cases.' Amanda glanced up as the front door swung open. 'Hi, Tom. I'll be standing in for Linda this morning.'

'Great!' Tom Kearney smiled warmly in response. Approaching sixty, Tom was a quietly spoken and gentle-mannered doctor who had lived in Ashburton for the last thirty years. His duties as an anaesthetist were not overly demanding and he managed to indulge and expand a passion for fishing that was locally renowned.

As the front door behind the anaesthetist opened again and Jack Armstrong entered, Amanda found the contrast startling. Even though Mr Armstrong had culled the waistcoat he still looked ready to step into a city boardroom. The relaxed atmosphere in the hospital foyer changed perceptibly.

'Hello, Jack.' Tom Kearney's greeting was warm. 'We've got a full list for you this morning.'

'Oh?' Amanda could see the spark of interest that brightened the dark blue eyes. The tight jaw muscles seemed to relax a little as well. 'What have we got?'

'Three tonsillectomies and two diagnostic D and C's.'

Amanda watched the spark die instantly. The face closed into an expression that bordered on disgust.

'It's a bit of a backlog,' Amanda explained. 'With not having had any surgery here for a while, we've got some catching up to do on non-urgent cases.'

'Do you ever have anything else?' The blue eyes locked accusingly on Amanda's.

Amanda tried to keep her tone friendly. 'I'll be assisting you this morning, Mr Armstrong.'

'Oh, wonderful. A midwife that doubles as a theatre nurse. I must commend you on your versatility.'

'Amanda's not a midwife,' Tom said calmly. 'She's our nurse manager. Second in command after Kevin Farrow.'

'Management?' Jack's expression was now as incredulous as his tone. Amanda bristled.

'I can find my way around a theatre quite competently if that's what's worrying you, Mr Armstrong.'

'Amanda can find her way around anything.' Tom's tone was also defensive. 'We count ourselves extremely fortunate that she's given Ashburton General the benefit of her capabilities and dedication for so long. We'd be having trouble coping with this flu if Amanda couldn't fill in where she's needed.'

'I'm sure.' The dark blue eyes scrutinised Amanda carefully but she ignored the glance.

'I'll come with you, Tom, while you check everybody. We're already set up for our first case.' Amanda's chin went up as she turned towards the surgeon again. 'We'll start the list at 10 a.m. Perhaps you'd like to accompany us and meet your patients?'

'I'll meet them soon enough.' Jack Armstrong

sounded disinterested. 'If there are any case notes available perhaps you can drop them into my office.'

Amanda and Tom Kearney exchanged a glance as Jack Armstrong strode away. Tom's eyebrow twitched and Amanda smiled without amusement.

'I think I might diagnose a slight attitude problem there.'

Tom Kearney grunted. 'Can't say I'm surprised.'

'Why is that?' Amanda asked curiously. She walked with Tom as he went to his office.

'I've known his father for a long time,' Tom said quietly. 'Or, rather, known of him in recent times. John Armstrong has kept to himself for many years now.'

'John Armstrong. I've never heard of him.'

'Oh, you must have. The family's been here for generations. Biggest farm in the district—or it was. John Armstrong got into terrible debt after he was nearly struck off and—'

'Struck off? Jack's father was a doctor?'

'Oh, yes. Here. Well respected, though I wouldn't say popular. I worked with him for years. Well before your time, of course. He officially retired about fifteen years ago but we used to call him in when we were short-staffed.' Tom Kearney pulled off his cardigan and reached for a rather crumpled white coat.

'What happened?'

'His wife walked out on him…oh, it must be twenty-five years ago. Took his only child with her. He started drinking. Nothing too serious until after he retired. There was a case…' Tom paused and then cleared his throat. 'It was a difficult period. I heard later that he'd lost the property but there must have been some agreement about the house because he's still there. There's been some ill-feeling in the district about that.'

Amanda lowered her voice. 'Why?'

'The farm itself got sold off even before I came—in the fifties, I think. It went into foreign ownership which didn't go down well with locals. It was a profitable farm and people thought the profits should be helping the local economy. John was left with just the house and a few acres. People had come to terms with the fact that the farm was gone but there's always been that underlying resentment.' Tom led the way out of his office. 'Selling the remaining part of the property to the same foreign company really stirred it all up again. There were even public meetings and a petition about it.'

'Why?' repeated Amanda, mystified at all the fuss.

'The house is listed with the historical society. An architectural treasure. There was a general feeling that it should be preserved and made use of in some way, instead of being allowed to crumble. The fuss has died down over the years but I expect it'll be renewed now. Jack's here on the understanding that his father is dying.'

'Armstrong. It's a fairly common name.' Amanda was trying to locate a piece of half-remembered hearsay.

'Ashcroft,' Tom prompted calmly.

'Ashcroft!' Amanda breathed out slowly. Her eyes widened dramatically.

Tom smiled wryly at her awed tone. He held open the ward door. 'Enough gossip, Nurse Morrison. Let's see if our young patients are looking forward to their ice cream.'

The children were still enjoying the novelty of their hospital admission. Six-year-old Jason Cotter, referred for surgery due to the recurrent tonsillitis he had suffered since the age of three, complicated by febrile convulsions, was the most boisterous. He wasn't interested in staying on his bed, especially while other children were in the playroom. With a lot of help from both his mother and Amanda, Tom gave him a thorough check. Satisfied that the boy was fit for an anaesthetic and that there was no active infection in either his ears or throat, Tom turned to the ward nurse with an amused expression.

'Time for a pre-med, I think, Colleen.'

Colleen barely suppressed a relieved sigh. 'I've got it right here.'

The other patients were much more co-operative. Ten-year-old Jane had had a frightening dose of quinsy last autumn which had required lancing under general anaesthetic. Not wanting to risk the chance of recurrence, her parents had been grateful to get her onto the waiting list for a tonsillectomy. Their third patient was a twenty-one-year-old, desperate for relief from a sleep apnoea condition which had led to him being fired from his builder's apprenticeship because he kept falling asleep on the job. Listening to his long history, which had finally led to diagnosis of the problem, Amanda found her thoughts wandering.

Ashcroft! The house was a local legend and had always been shrouded in mystery and more than a little magic as far as Amanda was concerned. The property had marked the turning point of the long rambles along the banks of the Ashburton river and down Althorpe Forest Road that Ralph had enjoyed in his younger days.

Mostly hidden from the road by a tall macrocarpa hedge, the majestic entranceway of a stone-walled bridge across the water-race, finished by ornate iron gates, had afforded a glimpse of the house through a forest of old trees. A vast, two-storied weatherboard mansion, Amanda knew it had been the largest private house ever built in the area. She had also believed it was still owned by descendants of the original settlers who had built the house in the 1860s. It was part of the landscape and local folklore.

Snippets of information had come her way over the years but it was always the house that was spoken of, never the owners. Amanda had assumed the house stood empty, imagined it to be sleeping—awaiting reawakening by new owners when its time came.

When Jack Armstrong appeared in the scrub room Amanda couldn't help staring at him with a new curiosity. He didn't seem to notice.

'What's that awful racket?' he snapped.

'Jason's decided it's not as much fun as he thought—being in hospital.' Even Amanda was impressed by the piercing shrieks coming from the anaesthetic annexe. 'He'd rather hang onto his tonsils.'

Jack was scrubbing with unnecessary vigour. Amanda watched the skin on his hands redden. The surgeon muttered an inaudible curse as he dried his hands.

'How long can it take to knock out a kid?' he said more loudly.

Amanda held out his gown. His tone brought yesterday's confrontation sharply back. She was still feeling disturbed by his attitude to Chloe and her baby. Did the man have any empathy with his patients at all?

'You're not keen on children, are you?'

'If I was keen on children I would have become a paediatrician.'

'I'm surprised you have an interest in obstetrics.'

'Purely a surgical interest.'

'That figures.'

'What is that remark supposed to mean?'

Amanda flushed slightly, more in embarrassment at her own unprofessional comment than as a response to the angry look and tone she had provoked. The exchange had been so rapid-fire her comment had simply popped out without her thinking about it. But she wasn't going to back down now. Jack Armstrong may as well be aware that at least one person didn't consider him to be God's gift to Ashburton General.

'I think your suggestion of removing Chloe Worbeton's baby yesterday before she had a chance to hold it was outrageous.'

'Both the girl and her mother were in a highly emotional state.'

'The birth of a baby often generates a strong emotional response,' Amanda shot back. 'It's considered normal.'

She may as well not have spoken. 'It had been made clear that the baby was going to be adopted. Any bonding that could occur in the time immediately after birth could only make the later separation more traumatic.'

'Rubbish! Avoiding the potential emotional repercussions can only intensify the trauma and make it last longer.'

'You're advocating that teenage mothers should all keep their children, then? Ruin their life prospects? What about the childless couples out there desperate to adopt?'

'I'm not advocating any such thing,' Amanda snapped. 'I'm just saying that the decision has to be an informed one. You're not going to solve the issues by stepping back into the Dark Ages and making an unplanned or unwanted baby simply go poof and vanish from its mother's life.'

To Amanda's surprise, Jack Armstrong laughed with genuine amusement. He shook his head. 'I find it hard to believe that you've managed to generate such a large amount of ill-feeling from a small difference of opinion.'

'A responsibility to consider the emotional well-being of patients is not a small issue.' Amanda drew herself up to her full height of five feet five inches. She still had to tilt her head to glare directly into Jack Armstrong's eyes. 'And I'm beginning to wonder just how far our difference of opinion might stretch. I understood you had returned to Ashburton because of a commitment to your own family responsibilities. Perhaps you don't extend the same commitment to your patients.'

His eyes darkened as he tied his mask. 'And what else have you heard, Nurse Morrison?'

Amanda reached for her own mask silently.

'I imagine the gossip machine is running full tilt,' Jack said sarcastically. 'It was only to be expected. Small town. Small minds.'

Amanda began to follow Jack into the theatre. She was seething. Jack stopped so abruptly as he turned that Amanda only just prevented herself from bumping into him.

'I have my own reasons for being here. They're none of your business. And I'm not going to be told how I should or should not behave by a nurse. Do I make myself clear?'

'Absolutely clear,' Amanda responded through gritted teeth. Clear that you're an absolute bastard, she added silently.

If Tom Kearney or the junior theatre staff had heard any of the scrub-room interchange they gave no indication. Tom was as calm and genial as always. The junior nurses were animated and more interested in the newcomer than the routine surgery.

Amanda assisted in total silence, passing instruments as requested but replacing them with a deliberate firmness, The muted clunk of the toothed forceps and the scalpel being returned to the draped trolley was followed by the sizzle of diathermy as the bleeding minor vessels were cauterised. She passed the suture material to tie off a larger blood vessel and then retrieved the soaked padding that had been placed to prevent blood spilling down the throat. Finally, she took charge of the wicked-looking stainless-steel gag that had been used to keep Jason's mouth open and his tongue out of the way.

Jack Armstrong stepped back from the table. He stripped off his gloves and then removed the headband holding the light which had been necessary to illuminate the dim operating field.

'Wake him up out of earshot, will you, Tom?' Jack

turned towards the scrub room without a word of thanks to Amanda or the other nurses. The juniors exchanged wide-eyed expressions but Amanda's lips tightened as she bundled the used instruments inside the soiled drapes. She was going to have a careful look at the rosters and availability of casual staff later that day, she decided. For once she would be happy to step away from practical nursing duties.

They were all short procedures. It took more time to set up, anaesthetise and then wake up the patients than to do the surgery. Amanda avoided any further conversation with Jack Armstrong by making sure she scrubbed first, directing one of the junior nurses to assist the surgeon with fresh gowns and gloves while she stood waiting in Theatre, her gloved hands held carefully away from her body.

The final case was over by 1 p.m. and Amanda hurried away. Dorothy would have already had her lunch but there might at least be time to share a cup of tea. The old woman had her tapestry frame on her knees. She was unwinding a length of pale green wool.

'Could you thread this needle for me, dear? I'm sorry, I think the tea might be cold by now.'

'It doesn't matter.' Amanda took the needle and wool. It amazed her that Dorothy was still able to do her handwork. The gnarled, shaky hands moved very slowly but the stitches were still placed perfectly and very even. It was a garden scene she was working on, quite an intricate arrangement of trees, flowers and birds, but the picture had grown significantly in the weeks Dorothy had been hospitalised. To Amanda's consternation, she found her own hands shaking as she tried to thread the needle. She must be more tense than she'd realised. Successful on the second attempt, she handed it back to Dorothy who was watching her carefully.

'Has it been a bad morning, dear?'

'It's going to be a bad three months, I expect,' Amanda responded gloomily. 'Did you know we have a locum surgeon now?'

'Have we? Oh, dear. I suppose I'll have to think about having my foot looked at now.' Dorothy frowned. 'Do you not think he's suitable?'

'He's quite competent. I think you might call it a personality clash. We've had a bit of an argument.'

'Oh, dear. When did he start work here?'

'Yesterday.'

'And when did you have the argument?'

Amanda had to smile ruefully. 'Yesterday. We managed to continue it this morning.'

'Not the best start, is it?'

'No.' To her own astonishment, Amanda felt her eyes fill with tears. She tried unsuccessfully to blink them away then fished in her pocket, also unsuccessfully, for a tissue. Dorothy passed her a freshly ironed handkerchief from her tapestry bag.

'He's upset you, dear,' she said with concern. 'What was it all about?'

Amanda blew her nose vigorously and stared over the verandah railing in silence for a minute. Dorothy McFadden waited patiently.

'I told you that you reminded me of my grand-mother, didn't I?'

'Many times, dear.'

Amanda looked around her. They were alone. She

took a deep breath. 'I got pregnant when I was seventeen, Dorothy. My parents disowned me. At least my father did and my mother didn't care enough to stand up to him. My grandmother offered to take me in so that was why I came to Ashburton. She supported me totally and I loved her for it. I could have kept the baby—she would have supported me.'

Dorothy's voice trembled more than usual. 'But you didn't keep the baby?'

There was another long silence as Amanda struggled with difficult memories. 'I never got the chance. She died just a wee while later.' Amanda blew her nose more carefully this time. 'I never even saw her…never held her.' She looked up at Dorothy and was surprised to see tears on the old lady's cheeks.

'Yesterday we had a teenager who had a baby. This new surgeon had to help with the delivery. He knew they were planning to have the baby adopted so he told me to take it away to the nursery—before the mother had a chance to hold it. I was angry.'

'Of course you were, dear. You were quite right to be angry.'

'We argued about it again today. I'm not sure I can work with him. I wonder if he has any idea at all of how his patients feel. Or cares about it if he does.'

'I don't think a man could ever understand the need to touch and hold a new life that has come from your own body.' Dorothy spoke softly and sadly. So softly that Amanda only caught the gist of her words. So sadly that Amanda was worried. She knew the old lady had no children of her own. Had she upset her too much by revealing her own sad story? She reached over and patted Dorothy's hand.

'I'm sorry. I didn't mean to upset you. If my grand-mother was still alive she would be the only person I could talk to about it who would understand. I shouldn't have burdened you.'

'I'm glad you did, Amanda.' Dorothy spoke more firmly. 'Did your young girl hold her baby yester-day?'

'Yes, she did.' Amanda smiled. 'So did her mother. I'm going to go and see her this afternoon. I want to make sure she knows she has plenty of support.'

Chloe was soundly asleep. The plastic bassinet beside her bed stood empty. The ward nurse directed Amanda towards the hospital gardens. She found Brenda Worbeton sitting on a comfortable bench, holding the newborn girl, an almost empty feeding bottle beside her. Amanda picked up the bottle and settled herself beside Brenda.

'How's the feeding going?'

'She seems to be accepting a bottle. We thought it was best if Chloe didn't try and feed her herself.'

Amanda nodded. She made a mental note to drop in on Chloe tomorrow. She could well remember the pain of pointlessly filled breasts after the milk came in. Brenda interpreted Amanda's silence as criticism.

'I only want what's best for Chloe,' she said de-fensively. 'I was pregnant at nineteen, only just twenty when she was born and I wasn't married. My family didn't want to know when I decided to keep the baby. I know what it's like to give up any am-bitions you have, to feel like you're missing out on everything. An interesting job, overseas travel—just going out to have a good time. And relationships. Do you have any idea how hard it is to find a genuine relationship when you've a child in tow? Especially in a small town like this.'

Amanda nodded sympathetically. 'I can imagine. But you've done something to be proud of, Brenda. You've raised a daughter on your own. She's a special person and your relationship with her is very important.'

'I don't regret keeping her, don't think that. In spite of everything she's the best thing that ever happened to me. But I don't want her to have the same regrets about what she's missed out on.'

'She would still have regrets. It's not something that can ever be forgotten,' Amanda said gently. 'The tie will always be there. Even when a child dies the mother will still live with it every day. She'll wonder about each milestone. Would she be smiling yet, have her first tooth, be learning to walk? Every birthday will be a time of regret and grief. In some ways it would be more difficult to know the child was still alive. It can be hard enough, seeing children you think are the same age or might look like your own child. What if you were haunted by the possibility that it might really be your own child?'

'That wouldn't happen. The adoptive parents are from Christchurch and we can keep in touch. The adoption system is much more open now.'

Amanda nodded. 'I'm not saying adoption isn't a good option. But Chloe needs to be informed about the repercussions and supported in whatever decision she makes. She's going to have to live with it for the rest of her life.'

'Don't I know it. Talk about history repeating it-self!'

'Not quite. There's an important difference be-tween you and Chloe.'

'What's that?'

'You had no family support. Chloe has you.'

'I'm too old to think about raising another child. Even part time.'

'How old are you, Brenda?'

'Thirty-five.'

Amanda smiled. 'There's a lot of women having their first babies at your age.'

Brenda returned the smile. 'Perhaps I just feel too old. It's all a bit much. The pregnancy was a terrible shock. Chloe didn't tell me until it was far too late to consider termination. And it was just a pregnancy. A disaster that we had to sort out and put behind us. But now…'

Amanda raised her eyebrows questioningly. Brenda gazed down at the sleeping bundle in her arms. 'Now there's a baby and she's beautiful. She's my daugh-ter's child. My grandchild. It would have been so much easier if we'd never seen her.'

'No.' Amanda shook her head firmly. 'No, it wouldn't, believe me.'

'But it's so hard!'

'Yes, it is. But you don't have to decide immedi-ately. You've got another week at least. Talk about it with Chloe, as much as she wants to. I'll make sure you both get some counselling from someone more qualified than myself. Don't rush any decisions. There are three people involved here and your decision will affect you all for a very long time.' Amanda stretched out a finger and lightly stroked the baby's downy scalp. Brenda's head jerked up.

'Goodness! What was that?'

Amanda had also heard the muted thump and then a drawn-out screeching sound. 'I've no idea.' They both sat, listening, but a peaceful silence had returned. Amanda shook her head. 'I'd better get back to work. Tell Chloe I'll come and visit later.'

Entering the hospital foyer, Amanda paused in surprise. One of the hospital's two physicians, Colin Garrett, was pushing a trolley laden with equipment towards the front doors. Seconds later one of the emergency department nurses ran past, carrying a portable defibrillator. The receptionist, Karen, was also staring at the activity.

'What's going on?' Amanda called.

Karen jumped and then turned, her face pale. 'There's been a terrible crash. A sheep truck has hit the Southern Express.'

Amanda was stunned. So that had been the unusual sound she and Brenda had heard. The Southern Express was the only passenger train that used the main trunk line. It was a popular form of transport these days. The casualties would be—

'Don't stand about, Nurse. You're needed. Follow me.'

Amanda was glad of the curt command. She ran to keep up with Jack Armstrong's loping stride. 'We'll take my car. They said it was the crossing near the tree nursery. Where's that?'

'Turn right,' Amanda directed. 'And then left. It's a couple of miles up the road.'

CHAPTER THREE

AMANDA had seen many horrific sights in her medical career but nothing touched the scale of the disaster she found herself in only minutes later.

The large, fully laden stock truck had ploughed straight into one of the train's passenger carriages. A gaping hole was framed by twisted metal, shards of glass and mangled seating. The carriage, still pinned to its companions, was partially derailed and rocking with the movement of terrified people trying to escape and rescue personnel trying to gain entry. Screaming and shouting seemed to come from all sides. The stock truck only added to the horror. The cab had been crushed, leaving little hope of its driver surviving, and the huge vehicle had then rolled. Maimed and bleeding sheep wandered through the scene, their panic-stricken cries blending with the sounds of human misery.

The local ambulance and fire service vehicles had already arrived. A policeman was trying to herd shocked, but uninjured passengers from the other carriages further away from the scene. Amanda found her hand firmly clasped.

'Come on.'

Jack towed her at a run towards the knot of people blocking the access to the damaged carriage but they were waved down by an ambulance officer.

'They've got to secure the carriage,' he shouted.

'It's going to tip right over if you get in now. Here, put this on.' He handed Amanda a fluorescent orange waistcoat with reflective strips and writing on the back. 'We need to have all medical personnel identified.'

'Thanks. Mr Armstrong will need one as well.' She saw the look the paramedic cast at Jack who had discarded the morning's theatre attire in favour of his pin-striped suit again. 'This is our new locum surgeon, Mr Armstrong, Robert. Mr Armstrong, this is Robert Bayliss, our paramedic.'

'Call me Jack.' The surgeon had stripped off his jacket and tie and was now rolling up his shirtsleeves. He reached for the bright waistcoat with the label of DOCTOR on the back. 'What's the protocol for dealing with a multiple casualty incident here?'

'Christchurch has been notified. Full emergency backup should be here within twenty minutes. Rescue helicopter is on the way and the air force is on standby.'

'Do we have any idea of serious casualty numbers?'

'Not yet. We'll have to get the minor injuries clear. There could have been forty people in that carriage. And there'll be others.'

The noise level seemed to be increasing. Fire service personnel were waving them over. People were being lifted from the carriage now. Colin Garrett was kneeling on the ground, pressing a bloodstained towel against an obvious arterial bleed on an unconscious woman's leg. Tom Kearney, carrying an oxygen cylinder in one hand and a drug kit in the other, disappeared into a huddle of people surrounding another

prone figure. Numerous passengers were sitting or lying, still conscious but immobilised by shock or injury.

'Over here, Doctor. We've got someone not
breathing too well.' The fireman held out a hand to
help Amanda up. 'Watch out for the glass,' he
warned.

It was difficult to climb over the mangled seating.
Amanda's foot caught on some metal piping and she
pitched forward. Jack caught her arm and steadied
her. Amanda eyed the shard of glass she'd narrowly
missed.

'Thanks.'

'Just watch your footing. We've got enough to deal
with here.' Jack already had his hand on a man's
neck. 'And, for God's sake, put some gloves on,
woman!'

The victim lay behind and beneath the seat Amanda
had tripped on. The lower half of his body was
trapped. His head was turned awkwardly to one side
and his breath sounds were harsh and obstructed. Jack
rapidly examined his head and shone a small torch
into each eye. He was crouched very uncomfortably
in the remaining aisle space.

'No obvious head injury,' he told Amanda, 'but his
breathing's obstructed.'

The fireman was behind Amanda. 'We can't get
him out until we get some more help.'

The harsh breathing sounds suddenly stopped.

'We'll have to intubate him,' Jack said. 'Hell of a
position. Pass me a laryngoscope, Amanda.'

Amanda was ready. Jack almost had to lie down to
get into a workable position. To one side of him a

stretcher was being manoeuvred over the top of the wreckage. Amanda squeezed back to let them get past but someone trod on Jack's foot. He grunted with pain but didn't look around, concentrating on his seemingly impossible task of inserting an airway with a correct alignment.

'Stethoscope.' Jack's arm twisted upwards and Amanda put the coiled instrument into his hand. Jack's hand, holding the disc, disappeared behind the seat back. 'Good,' he said a moment later. 'We've got air moving on both sides. Let's get an IV line in. Things are pretty tight in here. Could well be crush injuries.'

The sound of a helicopter muted the noise level from the people outside. A door further down the carriage was being forced open and a new level of confusion broke out within the carriage.

'Doctor, over here! Quick!'

Amanda took over the end of the cannula Jack had inserted into the man's arm. She connected the bag of haemaccel and opened the flow. Looking up, she saw a young policewoman staring at her. 'Hold this up,' she directed, passing her the bag of fluid.

Jack had not yet reached the area of the carriage where help was being called for. Amanda saw him crouched, unmoving, a little way along the aisle. She clambered towards him. What was he doing? For the space of a few seconds he seemed frozen. Having just coped so brilliantly, was he going to fall apart in the crisis now?

A shout was clearly heard from outside the broken window beside her.

'Someone call a vet. Get these bloody sheep dealt with.'

Amanda took another two steps to reach Jack. Looking over his shoulder, she gasped. The crumpled form of a very young child lay beneath the seat, a tiny upturned hand reaching towards them. Jack's voice was gruff.

'There's nothing we can do.' He looked up as he straightened. Their eyes met for only the briefest moment before he turned away but it was enough for Amanda to know that she had been very wrong about this man. He cared. He cared very much.

A young woman, possibly the child's mother, lay against the other side of the carriage. She, too, had died from her injuries. Paramedic personnel were lifting another stretcher from the doorway and cutting equipment was already being used to free the man they had just intubated. Clearly, the backup help had arrived in force.

Standing at the door of the carriage, Amanda found the scene outside had changed dramatically. A huge police vehicle, shaped like a furniture removal van, was obviously the centre of operations. Clearly identified paramedics, doctors and nurses from Christchurch were amongst the still swelling crowds of rescuers. The ambulance service had inflated a triage tent shaped like a long igloo and two stretchers were carried in as Amanda watched. She glanced down. The carriage was secure but still at enough of a tilt to make it quite a jump. Jack swung himself down with ease and glanced back to see Amanda's hesitation.

'Put your hands on my shoulders,' he ordered, turning back.

Amanda complied and then felt his strong grip on her waist as he swung her down. He let her go the instant her feet touched the ground but his eyes held hers for a second longer. They both looked away quickly, moving together towards the triage tent and the fleet of ambulances. A helicopter was taking off, another was coming in to land. Outgoing ambulances passed those coming onto the scene. Confusion had been replaced by a grim situation being dealt with by professionals. Onlookers were now being kept away by police tape. Even the sheep had been cleared from the scene, although some could be heard still trapped and panicked in the stock-truck trailer.

Outside the tent were whiteboards, listing the scene commander, incident officer, sector and triage officers. Patient details and totals were recorded as were the identities of ambulances being loaded or in transit. Inside, the scene was chaotic but controlled. Large plastic bins held stocks of IV and airway equipment, bandages, towels and oxygen masks. People were having limbs splinted, lacerations dressed and other injuries assessed.

Jack introduced himself to the scene commander.

'We've got two patients we're trying to stabilise,' he was told. 'You'd better get back to the hospital and get your theatre ready to go. I think we've got a ruptured spleen here.'

Jack was following the scene commander as he spoke. They stopped by a stretcher. The paramedic attending the patient glanced up. 'Left-sided injury. He was thrown across the carriage and landed against a door-handle. Lower ribs, upper abdomen. We've got abdominal distension and deteriorating respiratory effort.'

Jack looked at the two IV lines in place. The rapid fluid replacement was not going to be enough. 'Let's move,' he ordered. 'I'll travel with him.'

Amanda stood back as the stretcher was carried out. She saw Jack signal to Tom Kearney who came running and got into the passenger seat of the ambulance. The driver closed one half of the back door but Jack's head suddenly emerged from the other half.

'What are you waiting for, Amanda?' he called commandingly. 'Come on. I need you.'

Amanda Morrison was proud of the way Theatre staff rallied and coped with the emergency splenectomy. Life-saving, urgent situations were not as rare as they could have wished for in their small hospital but few were as dramatically messy as this. The large, high-pressure blood supply to the spleen through a five-branched artery meant that a huge volume of blood could be lost in a short time due to rupture. The pressure on the abdominal wall led to a fountain of blood over the entire operating field as Jack Armstrong made his initial incision. Two nurses assisted Amanda with suction equipment and gauze packs but it seemed as if Jack was trying to operate in a swamp of blood.

Colin Garrett was supervising the rapid and continuous blood transfusions. Tom Kearney had his hands full, monitoring a still falling blood pressure and deteriorating condition of their patient.

'More packs,' Jack ordered calmly. 'I need to get this colon out of the way.'

Amanda handed him the gauze packs that had been soaked in warm saline. The sleeves of Jack's gown were soaked in blood, even his goggles had been spattered. Amanda reached for the large clamp that she knew would be needed to hold the stomach. She peered over Jack's shoulder but could see nothing. He seemed to be operating purely by a sense of touch.

'I've got the ligament,' he told her. 'Scalpel, thanks, Amanda.' He handed it back quickly. 'We'll tie the smaller vessels in a minute,' he added. 'Right now I want to find this artery.'

Seconds later he requested blunt forceps and Amanda felt the tension ease just a little. He had located the splenic artery. Tied with a band of strong silk, the high-pressure blood supply to the spleen was finally halted. With no blood reaching it, the spleen began to shrink and the suction equipment was finally able to cope with the demands placed on it. Now Amanda could see what was happening. Jack still worked rapidly, cutting through the ligaments attaching the spleen to both the stomach and the left kidney. Clamping and tying off both the splenic artery and vein allowed the final removal of the badly damaged organ. The wound was then closed meticulously, blood vessels tied off or cauterised and each layer stitched separately.

'I wonder how they're getting on with the clean-up,' Jack remarked as he finished closing the abdominal wall. 'We may have some more customers waiting out there.'

'I'll go and have a look,' Colin offered. 'I think we've finally got enough of a circulation going here.'

Tom Kearney nodded his agreement. 'Looking good. BP's 110 systolic and rising.'

Colin was back as Jack was stapling the skin closed.

'There's quite a party going on out there,' he reported. 'Plenty of minor injuries waiting and one of the women's clubs is serving soup and sandwiches to all the local rescue teams. Apparently the other serious cases were airlifted to Christchurch. There's a television crew floating around as well.' He looked over at Amanda who was counting the used swabs and checking the tally again with the total written on the theatre whiteboard. 'X-ray and outpatient staff have all offered to stay on as long as they're needed but you might need some extras on night duty. I think we'll have a full house tonight.'

It was almost 8 p.m. by the time the last patient had been treated, discharged, transferred or admitted. Jack Armstrong stripped off his surgical gloves, wondering just how many pairs he had been through since scrubbing up for that first tonsillectomy that morning. Had it really been part of the same day? It seemed like another time and place. Had he really thought Ashburton had to be the most boring medical backwater in existence? Talk about variety. His resuscitation and diagnostic skills had been stretched more today than they ever had in the orderly environment of his old surgical routine.

He stretched his long frame, easing the ache in the small of his back. There were two fractures that still needed internal fixation—a broken ankle and a wrist—but they could wait until morning. Their owners were now well splinted and comfortable, tucked up in the surgical ward for the night.

Jack draped the white coat over his arm. Goodness knew where his suit jacket and tie were by now but he couldn't have cared less. Suddenly they also seemed to belong in another time and place. Leaving the emergency department, Jack strode down the corridor that led past the kitchens. Above the rattle of crockery being shifted he could hear the clear tones of Amanda Morrison's voice.

'You must go home, Mrs Golder. You've been brilliant but we're all under control now. Your feet must be killing you.'

'Ooh, they are at that, Mandy, but I just want to make sure we're going to cope with all the breakfasts.'

Jack veered through the open door. Amanda looked up. 'Did you need me, Jack? Sorry, I got a bit caught up with staffing arrangements. I do carry a beeper.'

'No, we're all done.' Jack turned away from Amanda and smiled at the large woman standing beside her. Mrs Golder was a wonderful advertisement for the desirability of the food she produced. 'You must be Mrs Golder,' Jack said. 'I hear it was you that was responsible for those delicious scones we had for morning tea.'

The cook beamed under the praise and the warmth of the smile she was receiving. She had known all those rumours about this man's unfriendly and unpleasant personality couldn't be true. 'How do you do, Mr Armstrong? I've heard a lot about you.'

'I'm sure you have.'

Amanda's eyes narrowed slightly but she couldn't

detect any hint of sarcasm. His smile could only be described as charming. 'Call me Jack,' he instructed. 'And what's this I hear about your feet giving you trouble?'

Mrs Golder flapped her hand. 'It's nothing, Jack. Just my age.'

Amanda shook her head. 'Mrs Golder has bunions. Quite advanced.'

Jack nodded. 'You'd better let me have a look some time,' he told the cook. 'I've done a bunion or two in my time.'

Mrs Golder shook her head. 'Nobody's getting near my feet with a knife.' Her face creased anxiously. 'I think I'll go home now, Mandy.'

'Thanks again for staying.' Amanda watched the older woman leave. The kitchen was now empty of its staff. She glanced at her remaining companion, her eyebrows raised. 'Touting for business, Mr Armstrong? I would have thought bunions would be about as exciting as tonsils.'

'Too much excitement isn't healthy,' Jack responded firmly. He caught Amanda's eye. 'We've had our fair share for a while after today.'

'It was a bit grim, wasn't it? Luckily it's not typical, though we do get some nasty car accidents a bit too often. Congratulations on that splenectomy. We were all very impressed.'

'So was I. With all of you,' Jack added hastily, seeing Amanda's expression. He looked around a little awkwardly. 'I don't suppose we could find a cup of coffee around here?'

'Help yourself,' Amanda suggested. 'I've got to go.

Ralph will be wondering where on earth I've got to. He'll be wanting his dinner.'

'Oh.' Jack's tone was unreadable. 'Is Ralph not capable of looking after himself, then?'

'No.' Amanda laughed. She wasn't going to enlighten him. 'Typical male, I guess.'

Jack took an hour, walking quietly around the darkened hospital after his coffee and making a check on all the new admissions. He knew he was putting off going home. The day had been extraordinary and he felt quite differently about his presence here now. Going home to that neglected, cavernous house and the unwelcoming company of his father, that could only plunge him back into the resentment and other unpleasant emotions he had fostered over the week.

Driving out of the hospital grounds, Jack still felt a need to avoid going home. On impulse he drew up outside the pub nearest the hospital on Willis Street. At least he could pick up a bottle of something that might make the situation more tolerable. Shivering in his shirtsleeves, Jack briefly thought again of his discarded suit jacket. It seemed appropriate in a way that he'd left it behind. The crisis marked a turning point, he could feel it. He could also feel the chill of the spring night. The warmth and noise of conversation from the public bar made Jack walk right through the bottle store without ringing the bell for service. He walked up to the bar and ordered a beer.

Conversation around him died suddenly and Jack could feel himself become the centre of attention. He gritted his teeth. Of course they were all interested in a newcomer. And one with a local history and a hint of past family scandal had to be a bonus. He nodded

politely at one or two people then spotted Tom
Kearney. Tom waved and Jack made his way through
the tables with relief. Amanda was sitting with Tom,
a young man beside her—presumably Ralph.

'Hi, Jack. This is Graham,' Amanda greeted him.
'Graham Baker.'

Jack raised an eyebrow. 'Where's Ralph?'

'I left him at home.' Amanda grinned. 'He's getting
a bit too old to enjoy going out at night.'

Jack saw the glance and smile exchanged between
Graham and Amanda. A look of understanding—and
friendship. Well, this sort of thing went on a lot in
small towns. He knew that. Still, he was a bit surprised about Amanda Morrison. She didn't look to be
that type at all.

'Graham's a vet,' Tom informed Jack. 'He had the
unenviable task of dealing with all those sheep this
afternoon. We all felt in need of a wind-down.'

Tom excused himself a short time later and when
Jack returned from the bar, carrying another beer for
himself and a glass of wine for Amanda, he found
her sitting alone.

'Graham had to get home,' Amanda explained.
'His wife needs a break from the baby at this time of
night.'

Jack gave a silent whistle. This was worse than
he'd thought. He knew it was none of his business
but something about this set-up suddenly angered
him. His tone was cool. 'How does Ralph feel about
Graham?'

He hadn't noticed the dimples in Amanda's cheeks
before. It gave her wide smile an impish quality. And
those dark brown eyes were fairly dancing with

amusement. 'Ralph adores Graham,' she told him enthusiastically. 'They all do.'

Jack's jaw dropped. Just how popular with husbands was this vet? 'They all do?' he echoed.

'Mmm.' Amanda took a slow sip of her wine. 'Not just the dogs. He's got a great rapport with cats, loves horses and can even get the odd stroppy goat to co-operate.'

Jack took a long swallow of his beer. The penny had dropped. With a surprisingly welcome clunk. 'Ralph's a dog?'

'Oh, yes.' Amanda's wide-eyed look belied her knowledge of the misunderstanding. 'A Gordon setter. He's quite old now, nearly eleven.'

'What kind of name is Ralph? For a dog, that is.'

'That's what he told me it was.'

'Excuse me?'

Amanda laughed. 'I got him as a puppy. He had this tinny little bark. You know, *rowf*! *Rowf*!' she imitated the sound. 'It got to be a bit of a joke. You'd say, "What's your name?" And he'd tell you. Ralph.'

Jack laughed. Really laughed. He felt the accumulated tension of the past week evaporate. For the first time he was actually enjoying himself. And enjoying the company of this vivacious young woman.

Suddenly he felt her hand on his arm. Instinctively, he drew back but Amanda wasn't looking at him. She was staring at the big-screen television set above one end of the bar. A late night news broadcast was on, with the coverage of the train accident taking priority. A silence spread through the room. The publican reached up and increased the volume. They all listened quietly, the horror of the incident refreshed by the images. Amanda looked away when a fireman was shown, climbing from the jagged hole in the side of the carriage, a small shrouded bundle in his arms. She knew what was inside that bundle.

She stared down at the table and tried to blink away the sudden tears, blotting out the sound of the media speculation into the cause of the accident and the review of other uncontrolled railway crossing disasters in recent times. When she felt a large hand envelop hers she returned the comforting pressure. Alone in that room, crowded with people, only she and Jack could share the pain of that particular memory.

A firmer squeeze on her hand signalled its release. But Jack's voice was soft. As comforting as the touch. 'You did a great job today, Amanda.'

'So did you,' she returned shyly. Then she smiled wryly. 'Not the best re-introduction to Ashburton for you.'

'Oh, I don't know,' Jack said thoughtfully. 'In some ways it's made me feel like I've really arrived. I've felt like a tourist until now.'

Amanda nodded. 'There's a big difference,' she agreed.

Did she mean a big difference for him? Or for herself in her opinion of him? He realised he had completely forgotten their acrimonious exchange that morning.

'I'm sorry about this morning,' he told her slowly. 'I guess I was still a tourist.' He watched her closely, wondering whether she understood.

This time Amanda smiled as she nodded. 'Apology accepted from Mr Armstrong.' She raised her wine glass in a toast. 'Welcome to Ashburton, Jack.'

*   *   *

Jack's stride was relaxed as he crossed the hospital reception area.

'Morning, Melissa!'

'Morning, Jack—and it's ''Mary'', remember?' The grin Marcia exchanged with Jack acknowledged that his initial disinterest in her name had become an enjoyable joke.

'Morning, Karen!'

'Morning, Jack!' Karen returned the smile eagerly and tilted her head so she could watch his progress a little longer, unconsciously smoothing back her blonde hair as she did so. Jack Armstrong had only been there for a week but he seemed quite a different person. Perhaps it was the clothes. The suit had long gone, replaced by comfortable, casual trousers and a leather bomber jacket over an open-necked shirt. It made him seem much younger and much more approachable.

Or perhaps it was the smile. A slow curve of a firm-looking mouth that made you feel as though you were really worth smiling at and he wasn't just being courteous. Or perhaps it was that brooding expression in those blue eyes. It made you want to know just what it was Jack was thinking about.

Jack exchanged the leather jacket for his white coat. Karen would have been disappointed to learn that his thoughts were, for the moment, entirely professional. He had a ward round to get on with, a full list for Theatre and an outpatient clinic that afternoon. It was routine on the surface but the last week had taught him to be prepared for anything—unexpected consultations with the physicians over one of their patients or frequent calls to the emergency department to deal with anything from a child swallowing a foreign object to an accident victim needing urgent surgery. The train crash last week had been an eye-opener.

He was in the front line here, with more responsibility and variety than he'd ever had to consider previously. It could have been a daunting prospect but Jack was revelling in the entirely unexpected challenge of his position. It was more than the distraction and time-filler he'd hoped for. It was, purely for its own sake, very satisfying.

Of course, the satisfying equation also included Nurse Amanda Morrison. With the staff absences from the flu tailing off he hadn't had the pleasure of her company in Theatre again or seen her in the obstetric department, but the advantage of the small hospital was that the staff encountered each other at frequent intervals even while engaged in quite separate areas. He didn't seek her out exactly, but he took advantage of the opportunities that presented themselves. And he watched, with interest, the way she interacted with the people around her.

Everybody loved her. Always smiling, ready to help, with a genuine concern for people that showed. And she was cute! Bouncy, black curls, dancing brown eyes and a round face that made you think she probably still looked exactly as she had when she'd been six years old. The rest of her didn't, mind you. 'Plump' wasn't quite the right word. He could remember exactly how firm her waist had felt when he'd swung her out of that train carriage. She was curvy, a woman's body that would be too slim if she were any taller. No, 'cute' wasn't the right word either. Amanda was too mature, too intelligent and far too capable to be thought of as 'cute'. She was...

With an irritated groan Jack pulled open the door of his office and strode off in the direction of the surgical ward. She was too damn attractive, that's what she was. The distraction of a woman had not been on the agenda when he'd applied for this position. It was like everything else around here. Surprises around every corner. Hidden challenges. Potentially life-changing considerations that he had no intention of being sucked into.

He had come to Ashburton with a single purpose— to exorcise the past and to do his duty. He would accomplish that purpose and then get on with his life. It was a brief sentence. But who could blame him if he was tempted to make it as tolerable as possible? Perhaps he should just ask her out. Get it out of his system. Find out if she found him half as desirable as he found her.

Jack's day became immediately more complicated with the first patient he saw on his ward round. Admitted two days previously for observation, thir-teen-year-old Wendy Page had suspected appendici-tis. Initially presenting with nausea, vomiting and constipation, dull central abdominal pain and a slightly raised temperature, the signs of inflammation were now much more evident. Wendy's temperature had shot up overnight and her pain had localised in the lower right-hand side of her abdomen.

Jack complimented the ward staff on having had the foresight to keep her nil-by-mouth since the pre-vious evening and he rearranged the theatre schedule to deal with Wendy's appendix as first priority. It was still possible that the girl was suffering a viral infection but Jack didn't feel comfortable waiting even the few hours it would take for fresh blood test results. He had no desire to see a young girl though a dose of peritonitis.

The rest of his ward round was brief. Two patients were ready for discharge and Tom Kearney had already checked on the cases for today's list. By the time Jack was scrubbed, Tom had Wendy induced and ready for surgery. Linda draped the girl's abdomen and then held out the forceps with the antiseptic-soaked pad which Jack used to swab the incision site. He made his initial incision two inches above the fold of the groin. He preferred to keep it as low as possible for girls in case they liked wearing bikinis for swimming. Boys were never as concerned about the possibility of a visible scar.

Holding the bleeding points with forceps, Jack waited while Linda sealed them with the diathermy probe. Together they used retractors to pull the skin edges and underlying fat apart and then split the layers of muscle beneath.

'Scalpel, thanks, Linda.' She was quick, Jack conceded, and she never fumbled, but she wasn't up to Amanda's standard. With Amanda, the instruments seemed to be in his hand even as he voiced the request. Jack shook his head imperceptibly as he exposed the intestines and began carefully extracting the whole caecum. He wanted to avoid even touching the appendix while it was capable of bursting and releasing a jet of infective material into the abdominal cavity. He also wanted to avoid any distraction caused by thoughts of Amanda Morrison.

'Suture, thanks.' Jack tied off the dangerous-looking appendix and cut it free. Then he placed a pursestring suture around its base, pulling it tight to close up the wall of the caecum and pushing the stump inside with the end of a pair of forceps. Now the caecum was returned to the abdominal cavity and he began the task of closing the wound.

'OK.' Jack finally stepped back and stripped off his gloves. 'Who's next, then?'

Amanda's day was proving as busy as Jack's but she made a point of keeping an hour free that afternoon. She had promised Dorothy McFadden she'd provide moral support when the first television interview was scheduled.

'How is she?' Kevin Farrow asked Amanda anxiously. He had left the small media team to set up their equipment out on the verandah.

'Fine,' Amanda responded. 'So far.'

'What do you mean?' Kevin frowned. 'You don't think it's possible she won't last till New Year, do you?'

'Seventy-five days is a long time when you're ninety-nine,' Amanda said mischievously but then she relented. 'I meant she's quite happy with all the attention so far. But I'm keeping an eye on things carefully.'

'I've got a women's magazine interested now,' Kevin said. 'They'd like an interview and photographs as well. They mentioned something about a donation to the hospital for the privilege.'

'Let's see how this one goes,' Amanda suggested

firmly. Then she laughed. 'No one can say you don't try, Kevin.'

Dorothy McFadden did seem to be enjoying the attention. Her silvery but thinning hair had been carefully brushed. A rug was arranged neatly over her knees and the producer had been delighted with the soft woollen shawl Dorothy had draped around her shoulders.

'Perfect,' she claimed. 'Now, keep your sewing in your lap. In fact, you can do a stitch or two while you're talking. We want a nice relaxed atmosphere. Let's get some fresh water in that teapot. I want to see a good curl of steam.'

Finally, they were ready. Amanda positioned herself quietly with several other interested onlookers. She hoped someone was keeping an eye on Jim Cooper. The old farmer had been known to remove all his clothing, with the exception of his hat, and appear in unexpected places. It would not be an example of geriatric care that Kevin Farrow would want to have made public. She tuned back into the conversation being recorded. Amanda knew something of Dorothy's history. Born in Scotland on New Year's Day 1900, she had been the youngest of eleven children. Her mother had died shortly after her birth and she had gone into service at the age of only ten.

'What brought you to New Zealand?' asked the interviewer.

Dorothy spoke quietly. Her words were considered, her thoughts carefully ordered. Amanda already had the impression that the interviewer wanted more direct answers to her questions but Dorothy wasn't go-

ing to be hurried. Amanda hoped the later editing of
the programme wouldn't be upsetting to its subject.

'I started work as a scullery and kitchen maid. I
started to work upstairs when I was fourteen. It was
quite a promotion. I always tried to do a little more
than was expected of me. Too much sometimes, I
think, but I was considered an excellent servant.'
Dorothy paused. The interviewer tried to redirect her
apparently wandering reminiscence.

'But this was in Scotland, yes? When did you come
to this country?'

'I was getting to that, dear. My employers had
friends who had come here with the first settlers. They
had a large property and house and were having difficulty finding enough staff, especially after the war
started. We heard that they were offering to pay the
passage for anyone with a good service record willing
to come and work for them. I was sixteen then. Ready
for an adventure.'

'And was it?'

'I beg your pardon, dear?'

'Was it an adventure?'

Dorothy nodded slowly. 'It was a significant chapter in my life. A short one. I returned to Scotland only
two years later.'

'Why was that?'

But Dorothy appeared not to have heard. She bent
her head over her tapestry frame and carefully pushed
the needle through the selected hole. The interviewer
glanced around her. Then she consulted the notes she
held. 'You've only recently returned to New Zealand.
What made you choose Ashburton?'

Amanda felt the change in atmosphere around her.

A collective sharpening of attention. The girl's tone made it clear that it had been an unlikely preference. But Dorothy smiled almost secretly.

'Well, dear. This was where it all started. I felt a need to revisit before it was too late. It was a missing section, don't you see? I wanted to see if I could fill any of it in.'

'I don't understand.' The look the producer received made Amanda realise the interviewer wasn't too convinced that Dorothy still had all her marbles.

'Look at this.' Dorothy shakily held up her needlework. 'I see my life—everybody's life—in this.'

The interviewer nodded a little wearily at the cameraman who changed angles slightly to zoom in on the emerging garden scene.

'Life is like needlework,' Dorothy explained slowly. 'Everything you do puts more stitches into the picture. We make mistakes but we can't undo them. If they're only small it doesn't matter. The whole picture is very large. What does matter is if you don't get enough colour.' Dorothy's voice trembled. Amanda could see she was tiring and stepped forward to wind up the session. But Dorothy had more she wanted to say.

'The worst thing is the empty spaces. Lost opportunities, unfinished business. Sometimes, if we're lucky, we get the chance to go back. To add a final touch of colour and maybe make an empty space less noticeable. That's why I came to Ashburton. But maybe I left it too late.'

To Amanda's horror, she saw a tear track its way down one of the deep wrinkles on Dorothy's cheek.

'We'll have to stop for now,' she said firmly. 'Miss McFadden is getting tired.'

Dorothy didn't seem to notice the activity around her as people dispersed. Amanda waited, intending to talk to Dorothy and make sure she hadn't been too tired or upset by the interview. She would be happy to cancel tomorrow's appointment if necessary. The producer was the last to leave. She stopped to thank Dorothy and admire her needlework.

'I like your philosophy,' she told the old woman. 'I think a lot of people will identify with it. I hope you can tell us more next time. About your own colours. About the gaps. Do you mean perhaps your regret that you didn't have any children?'

Dorothy shook her head. 'The gaps are private,' she said. 'Only you know if they're really there. If you let other people see them then sometimes they can't see anything else.'

The producer looked nonplussed. She opened her mouth to ask another question but then looked startled as Jim Cooper suddenly appeared and marched across the verandah towards her.

'What are the bloody wool sacks doing outside the barn?' he demanded angrily. 'Can't you see it's going to rain?'

Amanda bit back a smile as she grasped the old man's arm securely. 'Somebody's coming to shift them, Mr Cooper. Don't worry, I'll sort it out.' She began to lead him away but glanced back at the dazed-looking woman Jim had shouted at. 'It's the laundry bags,' she explained. 'They look like wool sacks. Jim lost his electric shaver when he put it in-

side one last week. He thought it was his shearing
handpiece.' Amanda gave her charge's arm a reassuring squeeze. At least Jim had kept his clothes on
this time.

CHAPTER FOUR

IT WAS really rather acutely embarrassing.

Brenda Worbeton was sitting opposite Jack's desk in the outpatient examination room, her daughter Chloe beside her. The baby lay asleep in its car seat positioned close to her chair. They were both eyeing him with suspicion and Jack knew it was quite justified. He had been insensitive at their first meeting. He had definitely been rude to Brenda whom he had remembered quite clearly and had brushed off, hoping to escape the sudden tug into his past. He hadn't even been back to see them after the delivery or enquired about the baby's fate. Obviously, they had changed their minds about the adoption.

Chloe was here now for the formality of the six-week postnatal check. An internal examination reassured Jack that her pelvic floor muscles were regaining their tone and that the bladder and uterus were still correctly aligned. The episiotomy scar had healed well. He could detect no evidence of postnatal depression in his conversation with the teenager but a query regarding future contraceptive requirements earned him a withering look. Tactfully, Jack changed the subject, deciding to ensure that his follow-up letter to Chloe's GP underlined the need to educate and protect the young mother from a repeat performance.

Leaving Chloe to get dressed again in privacy, Jack

found himself sitting alone with Brenda. He broke the silence before it could become too uncomfortable.

'I do remember the mouse, Brenda. It was you that dobbed me in. I got the strap for that.'

'I never did!'

'But you were the only person who saw me do it. You thought it was a great joke.'

'I also saw Mrs Allen checking everybody's desk at lunchtime. I knew your desk smelled funny. How long had you had the mouse in there?'

Jack grinned. 'A week or two. I guess it *was* fairly obvious. OK, I give up my long-held grudge.'

'I've never heard anyone scream that loudly ever since. I've never forgotten.'

'I had, until you reminded me. It was a long time ago.'

'Chloe went to the same school. It kept a lot of memories alive for me. Like that dog of yours that used to wait by the school gate for you every day.'

'Gypsy.' Jack's smile was poignant. 'She was a good friend. It was a long walk home every day.'

Chloe emerged, straightening her skirt. Brenda glanced at Jack curiously. 'Have you got any children, Jack?'

'I never married,' Jack said simply.

'Didn't stop me.' Brenda sighed. 'And here I am a grandmother. And a mother all over again.'

Jack raised an eyebrow.

'We couldn't give Lucy away in the end but I was determined that Chloe wouldn't lose her opportunities the way I did. So I'm adopting Lucy. Officially I'll be her mother. Chloe's gone back to school. Maybe she'll go to university or find a good job. Maybe she'll want to raise Lucy herself later. I'll support her whatever she chooses. Life goes in a circle sometimes, doesn't it?' Brenda stared at Jack thoughtfully. 'And here you are, back in Ashburton after all this time.'

'Only temporarily,' Jack said hastily. Then he gave a rather surprised smile. 'I must confess I'm rather enjoying it now.'

In fact, the enjoyment of being here had increased markedly in the last two weeks, ever since he had given in to his inclinations and invited Amanda Morrison out to dinner. Her initial reluctance had been expected and Jack had entered into the spirit of the game with more enthusiasm than he'd felt for a long time. It had only added to a sweet sense of victory at her acceptance a couple of days later. The food and wine at the restaurant had been surprisingly up to an international standard. And the company had been stimulating in more ways than one. It was really rather delicious, this intense attraction, without pushing it any further. Jack was sure it was returned, though perhaps not to the same degree.

The dinner had been followed by a walk early last Sunday morning. This time the invitation had come from Amanda and Jack had been delighted to meet Ralph. The gentle, dignified dog had walked glued to Amanda's side and Jack had experienced a vivid reminder of the pleasures of rural springtime walks with a devoted canine companion. They'd all explored the large domain in the town centre but Jack had been unprepared for the tug of childhood memories.

'I played rugby on that field every Saturday morning,' he told Amanda excitedly. 'After a good frost the ground was like iron. Made the ball bounce a treat but it was hell on the knees. And that field over there—that was the one the circus got set up on when it came to town. We used to sneak away from school to watch the animals.'

They crossed a rustic bridge over a duck pond and stopped to watch a pair of magpies making use of an old stone birdbath.

'You know, I hadn't realised I'd missed magpies until I heard one cawdling the first morning I was back. It's a completely unique sound.' Jack had looked towards the rose garden as the magpies flew away. 'Who's buried under that tree?'

'It's not a tombstone,' Amanda told him. 'It's a memorial put up by the mayoress in September 1910 after the death of Florence Nightingale. She died on August the tenth.'

'You have amazing eyesight. I'm impressed.'

Amanda laughed. 'I don't need to read it. I know what it says by heart. It's what made me decide to take up nursing. I used to come here all the time when Ralph was a puppy and I was wondering what life had to offer.'

Jack moved closer to the huge slab of stone. 'Fancy having a mayoress in 1910,' he commented. 'Quite forward thinking, weren't they?'

'Perhaps they still are.'

Jack snorted dubiously. 'Have you looked around lately?'

'How do you mean?'

'It's typical small-town New Zealand. One main street, an incredible mishmash of architectural styles in dilapidated old buildings. Faded signs for tearooms and fish-and-chip shops. A couple of pubs and the regulation war memorial, of course. Oh, and one set of traffic lights!'

Amanda laughed again. 'We've got four traffic lights, thank you. Two on East Street and two on West Street. And it's not what the place looks like that's important. It's the people that count.'

'Right. And I could count them in no time flat.'

'We've got about fifteen thousand in the town,' Amanda informed him. 'And the hospital services cover a population of at least twenty-five thousand.'

'You can't even see the sea. It's flat and boring. I'll bet the circus hasn't even been back since 1972.'

'There's plenty of excitement,' Amanda said defensively. 'Try a balloon safari, white-water rafting, heli-skiing and tramping. It's all within easy reach if that's what you want.'

'No, thanks, I'm not a tourist.'

'You sound like one,' Amanda pointed out. 'You're only looking at the surface and what it's got to offer you.'

'It hasn't got anything to offer me,' Jack said quietly. 'Maybe…if my father hadn't thrown Ashcroft away, there would have been something worth coming back for.' The bitterness showed all too clearly in his face.

Amanda thought of Jack's unsatisfactory relationship with his father. 'Perhaps there still is,' she suggested gently.

Jack smiled at her earnest tone and the expression in those dark eyes. His face softened and he raised his hand to stroke her cheek in a quick gesture to acknowledge her sympathy.

'Perhaps there is,' he agreed, still smiling softly. 'I guess I'll keep looking for a while longer.'

Jack knew he didn't have to look any further. It had been staring him in the face for weeks now. And all the time the desire grew. Jack worked through the rest of the outpatient clinic with an increasing sense of background urgency. He had been holding back partly because of the unexpected strength of that desire. He wasn't going to be here for long. What right did he have to push himself intimately into the life of someone who obviously had no desire to leave an environment that was too suffocating for him?

If Amanda wanted something that could only be short-lived that was fine, but he needed some indication that that was what she did want. He could see the way she reacted when they met each other at work, could sense the welcome and enjoyment of his company away from the hospital. They could laugh now about their initial impressions of each other. The friendship was there but not quite trust yet.

And Jack wasn't ready for that. He had managed until now without trusting a woman. It was no barrier to a great physical relationship. The anticipation was getting a little too close to frustration now, however. Maybe after this outpatient clinic was over with he would go and find Amanda. He'd drop a broad hint and see what her reaction might be.

Ethel Golder failed to keep what was the second outpatient appointment Jack had sent her through the internal mail system. He smiled and made a note to send her a third appointment card. He rather enjoyed prodding her nervousness about surgery and dispensing the reassurance she craved. This time he would deliver the card personally and make sure that Mrs Golder really understood how the correction of her foot deformity could add to her quality of life.

The last outpatient for the day was Donald Fisher. A young farmer, he was acutely embarrassed by the reason his GP had referred him to the clinic. Jack tried to be matter-of-fact after perusing the GP's letter.

'You left it for quite a while, did you, Donald?'

'Yeah. It was a bit…you know…'

Jack nodded. 'Size getting to be a bit of a problem now, though?'

'I play rugby. On Saturdays. Local A grade.'

'Congratulations. You must be good.'

'Got a bit of a knock a couple of weeks ago. Hurt like hell.'

'I'll bet.'

'And there's the changing shed, too. A mate told me I looked like Jefferson.'

'Jefferson?'

'My prize bull.' Donald's face had reddened alarmingly but he summoned enough courage to meet Jack's eye at that point. They both laughed and the tension was broken.

'Let's have a look, Donald. A sliding hernia is a pretty straightforward repair job. Only day surgery. Your scrotum size will reduce pretty quickly once we fix up the problem.'

At last the clinic was over. Jack found Amanda in her office. Large sheets of paper were spread on her desk and a frown creased her face.

'Everybody wants New Year's Eve off. Looks like you and I will be the only staff available.'

'Suits me. I reckon we could cope with anything.' Jack leaned over her desk and lowered his voice to a husky drawl. 'Maybe we can have our own party.'

The dark brown eyes glinted at the obvious invitation. Was it just a response to his flirting that made the tip of a pink tongue appear and sweep sensuously across her lower lip? Whatever the reason, his reaction was painfully intense. He eased back from the edge of the desk.

'Are you sure you don't want Christmas Day off?' Amanda sounded breathless. 'To be with your father?'

Jack flicked his hair back from his forehead as he straightened reluctantly. He hadn't scored well with that attempt. 'I've told you, he doesn't like me being around too much. He's getting used to it but I can't see any major family celebration being planned. He thinks I'm only here to collect my inheritance and he's in no hurry to hand it over. Not that there's much to collect now, anyway. I suppose, if I'm honest, the idea of inheriting the house was the main reason I came but if it was the only reason I'd be long gone. He made sure I knew that it was no longer mine to inherit the day I arrived.'

Amanda dropped her eyes. She hadn't meant to remind him of his loss of Ashcroft. 'It's a while off, anyway.'

'Forty-one days, and counting. I swear that whiteboard gets bigger every day.'

'The streamers will be out soon,' Amanda warned him. 'Karen and Marcia are loving it. It's certainly giving everybody something to look forward to.'

'Which reminds me.' Jack moved in for another

attempt. 'Can I take you out to dinner again on Friday? I'd like something to look forward to myself. Especially on a Friday night.'

'Not Friday.' Amanda looked encouragingly disappointed. 'That's the Young Farmers' Association barn dance.' Then she brightened. 'Why don't you come? It's always great fun. Everybody goes. It's a real community get-together.'

'Hmm. Not quite my scene. Let's make dinner Saturday and I'll pass on the barn dance. I'm too much of an outsider.'

Amanda was giving him a peculiar look. 'You might think you are, Jack. You might want to be. But you might be very wrong, you know.'

Wrong about what? Being an outsider or wanting to be one? It was an irritating suggestion which had preoccupied him all evening. Even this morning, with a busy day surgery schedule ahead of him, Jack hadn't quite shaken it off. Of course he was right. On both counts.

Donald Fisher was the first case for the day. The incision in the crease of his groin was deep enough to cut through the skin and underlying fatty tissue. The veins were severed and tied off, then Jack cut through the layer of tendon to reveal and free the outer fibres of the spermatic cord. Now he could pull free the protruding loop of bowel and replace it in the abdominal cavity. He then turned his attention to reinforcing the weak point of the abdominal wall that had caused the hernia. Even with the sterile mesh he was using for additional strength, Donald was going to have to be careful to avoid a recurrence of the

problem. Rugby was going to be a risky pastime. And
the young farmer certainly wouldn't be feeling like
attending the barn dance on Friday evening.

Why had he decided to come himself?

To prove a point, that's why. To show Amanda
Morrison he was right. Besides, it was the only way
he was going to get to see her and he didn't want to
wait until their planned dinner date tomorrow. The
days on Karen's whiteboard were ticking past. If he
didn't do something he might find himself on a plane
back to London without ever finding out whether such
an expectation could possibly measure up to reality.

The hall was packed. Hundreds of hay bales had
been stacked to provide the seating. Beer was being
dispensed from kegs, a huge barbecue was set up in
the corner, the smell of frying sausages pervasive.
And the noise! The raised stage at one end of the hall
was the setting for a scene Jack had trouble believing.
The band were all geriatric! The chap playing the
violin looked at least ninety years old and it had to
be his twin giving the raucous calls to the dancers.
But they were belting out their rendition of 'Cotton
Eye Joe' with impressive skill and the formations of
dancers on the floor were clearly having a ball.

'Jack!' The yell came from the nearest set. The
dancers skipped down the middle of the two lines and
through an arch being made by the leaders' arms. One
of the arch supports was being made by Amanda. Her
black curls were scrunched into two pigtails, unnat-
urally large freckles had appeared over her upturned
nose and her denim dungarees were rolled up to her
knees. The toenails on her bare feet were painted scar-

let. She looked like a child. And a very happy one at that.

'Come on, Jack!' His hands were grasped firmly and he was pulled in as the group of people reformed a square. He saw Graham Baker mopping his brow and heading off in the direction of the beer kegs. Jack must have replaced him as Amanda's partner but the young vet didn't look at all bothered. Amanda showed no signs of tiring. Her instructions were shouted to him along with the caller's and it was hard to hear either over the stamping, clapping and cat calls of the enthusiastic participants.

'You wouldn't get a do like this in London, I bet!' Amanda shouted as they twirled, arms linked, at the edge of a circle. 'No! Don't follow me. You go *that* way!'

But Jack had undermined the whole group's concentration by taking the opposite direction. Confused, they bumped into each other and then, laughing, they gave up and stood back to clap and cheer the groups still in action. The song finished and even the band took a refreshment break.

'You left it a bit late, Jack. It's nearly time for the bangers and mash.'

'I wasn't even going to come, remember?'

'I remember.' Amanda clambered up a stack of hay bales to sit on the top. Jack stood one level down, looking at his feet, trying to assess the stability of the stack.

'Hey, Jack?' He lifted his head at the quiet call and found his face close to Amanda's.

'I'm glad you did.'

'Did what?'

'Come tonight.' She was watching him closely, her eyes shining, her smiling lips parted a little.

'Me, too. But thanks.' Jack leaned closer. The invitation was irresistible. As his lips touched Amanda's the original intention of an appreciative gesture exploded into something he couldn't begin to recognise.

How long had it been since someone had kissed her like this? Never. Amanda wound her arms around Jack's neck, oblivious to their surroundings. She had never been kissed like this in her life. The pull of desire she had been enjoying for the last few weeks became a tight knot. As she felt the heat of his tongue against hers the knot branched painfully, sending shock waves into her thighs. His mouth was very gentle but the pressure kept ebbing and then returning with increasing insistence as though the exploration of her lips and mouth were only the initial step of a journey intended to become much longer.

It was the cat calls that made them surface. Or, rather, the single, gleeful shout that finally penetrated the cloud of desire.

'Way to go, Doc!'

Amanda and Jack pulled apart, gave each other a long and stunned gaze and then both turned to see Donald Fisher standing at the base of the haystack, grinning up at them. And he wasn't the only one. Hoots of appreciation erupted. Someone yelled for an encore and then the clapping started. Amanda blushed a fiery red but Jack gazed around at their audience. There was no malice there. He could see a lot of people and he could also see they felt a genuine interest and pleasure that one of their community was obviously enjoying herself. Jack grinned down at them.

'I'm beginning to feel right at home,' he called. 'Take an aspirin and don't call me in the morning.'

The appreciative response was curtailed by a loud clanging. The chief chef was banging a ladle on the side of the huge kettle of mashed potatoes.

'Come and get it, folks. You'll need plenty of stamina. The dancing's only just begun!'

Jack grinned again as he saw how carefully Donald Fisher was walking towards the supper table. He was still smiling as he looked back at Amanda.

'Are you on for the bangers and mash? Can I get you a beer?' He paused at the expression in her brown eyes and moved his face a little closer. 'Or is there something else you want?'

Amanda swallowed hard and then nodded, the power of speech almost deserting her. She cleared her throat. 'Not here,' she whispered huskily.

'No.' Jack agreed with a lopsided smile. 'Not here.' He took her hand and helped her climb down from the hay bales. As they turned away from the supper table towards a less obvious fire exit a large figure emerged from the crowd.

'Jack! Yoo-hoo, Jack!'

Mrs Golder was an extraordinary sight in denim jeans. She was hobbling painfully towards them in a pair of black gumboots.

'Jack, dear. I've made up my mind.' With a sigh of relief, Mrs Golder sat down heavily on the nearest hay bale and began to ease off a gumboot. 'You can look at my bunions,' she told Jack generously. 'I'm fed up with not being able to dance any more.'

*   *   *

It was Dorothy who spotted the change in Amanda on Monday. The old woman had been unusually talkative, telling Amanda about the interview for a women's magazine that had been conducted that morning.

'They wanted to know about all the changes I've see this century. Whether I thought they were good or bad.'

Amanda was checking over the trolley she had brought with her into Dorothy's room. 'What did you say?'

'Like everything else, there's always a good side and a bad side. The pace of life has become too fast for me. People expect everything instantly. They forget that the really good things still take just as much time as they always have.'

'Such as?' Amanda selected the dressing pack she required and pulled out a fresh mask and gloves from their slotted boxes.

'Friendship. Love. Raising children. Growing a garden.' Dorothy was watching Amanda wash her hands. 'Some things don't change.'

'Let's hope this is changing a bit.' Amanda checked the lower limb pulses at four points before removing Dorothy's dressing, scoring 0 for normal, 1 for a diminished pulse and 2 for the absence of a pulse. Dorothy's left leg had a marginal score of 3. Any higher would have indicated that the blood supply was inadequate for healing and in a younger patient would have led to referral for vascular surgery. Amanda tied on a mask, put on the gloves and removed the dressing on Dorothy's left heel. So far they had managed to keep the ulcer clean and free from infection. It should have been reducing in size by at least a third every fortnight. Amanda measured the lesion and her heart sank as she confirmed no change since the last measurement.

'I'm going to get the surgeon to come and look at this tomorrow,' she told her patient. 'It may be possible to try a skin graft. It's not healing quickly enough and I don't want to keep you immobilised any longer. Sorry.' Amanda's face creased in sympathy as Dorothy winced at her touch.

'What's he like, this new doctor?'

Amanda could feel the prickle of heat in her cheeks. 'He's…um…he's very nice.' She avoided meeting Dorothy's eye as she reached for a fresh dressing. That had to be the understatement of the century, she admitted silently. The barn dance had disintegrated into rather a farce with the public interest in Jack's surgical opinion of Mrs Golder's bunions. It had been too hilarious to sneak away after that and they had stayed dancing until the bitter end which hadn't been until 4 a.m. Their exhaustion had been enough to make Jack send Amanda home alone.

'You're too tired for what I have in mind for you,' he had warned Amanda. Then he had grinned disarmingly. 'Besides, think of the damage to my ego if you fell asleep while I was making love to you.'

Thank goodness it had been a Friday night. Amanda would never forget the tension of their dinner together on Saturday. She would never remember the food that had been placed in front of her and doubted that she'd even tasted it. They had both known what was coming after dinner and they had both revelled in drawing out the anticipation just that much further. Until it had been totally unbearable. And thank goodness it had been a Saturday night when they'd started because it had taken until Monday morning before either of them felt the introduction to each other's bodies had been completed to their satisfaction.

Amanda concentrated hard on the tricky task of fitting the sticky dressing neatly over the rounded shape of the heel. When she finally looked up she found Dorothy staring intently at her and she blushed all over again.

'Ah,' Dorothy said slowly. 'I'm very pleased he's so nice, dear. It's about time.'

'It is?'

'Of course. It's time you began putting some more colour into your life.'

'My tapestry, you mean?' Amanda gently lifted Dorothy's leg and propped her foot up so she could wind the crêpe bandage over the dressing. 'I'm very happy, Dorothy. But I was very happy with the way things were, too.'

'You've spent a long time being a part of other people's pictures, Amanda. You need something of your own. Something that can grow.'

'Maybe you're right.' Amanda's dimples appeared as she smiled. 'Maybe I've been waiting for a new direction. Something that won't remind me of the past.'

'You can never escape the past, dear. The stitches can't be undone. You have to learn to use them if you can. To make them part of the whole picture.'

'Is that what you're doing?' Amanda asked gently. She was still curious about the 'gaps' Dorothy had spoken of in her first interview but didn't want to pry into something private. 'Is that what brought you back to Ashburton?'

'It was my intention. But I've left it too late. There's not enough time left to include it. I'm afraid my picture is complete.'

'Not quite.' Amanda was packaging the soiled dressings. 'We'll get this foot better and you'll be able to get out of hospital. I'll talk to Mr Armstrong right now.'

'Who?'

Amanda glanced up, surprised at Dorothy's horrified whisper. 'Jack Armstrong. Our new surgeon.'

'Where has he come from? Why didn't you tell me his name?'

Amanda noticed Dorothy's agitation with concern. 'Don't be upset, Dorothy. I'm sorry I hadn't told you. He's here from London to visit his father who's very ill and may be dying.'

'Dying?' Dorothy closed her eyes suddenly. She looked pale—almost grey. 'John.' Her voice quavered. 'John Arthur Armstrong.'

'That's right.' Amanda was watching Dorothy carefully. She laid her hand over the frail wrist to feel for a pulse. 'Jack's name is the same as his father's and his grandfather's. Apparently his mother hated the family tradition and insisted he was called Jack instead.'

Dorothy's eyes flicked open. Amanda felt the pulse jump beneath her fingers. 'What else has he told you?'

'Not much. He doesn't talk about his father a lot. It sounds as though he's a rather unhappy man. Jack's mother left him many years ago and took Jack back to her relatives in England. Are you feeling all right, Dorothy? Did the dressing change hurt more than usual? I think I'd better get Dr Garrett to come and see you.'

'No. I'll be fine. Just leave me alone, dear.'

'I'll just take your blood pressure.'

'No!' Dorothy's tone was unusually curt. 'I'm tired, Amanda. I want to rest. Just go away.'

Puzzled and more than a little concerned, Amanda rang Colin Garrett anyway. By the time the physician arrived and they both went to see Dorothy, the old lady seemed to have recovered. She apologised for snapping at Amanda when Colin had finished his examination.

'I don't know what it was that upset me, dear. Perhaps it's the thought of having the surgery on my foot.'

'Dr Garrett seems to think there are some other things we can try before we resort to surgery,' Amanda reminded Dorothy. Amanda knew that Kevin Farrow would be all in favour of extending the hospital stay even further but avoiding surgical procedures in someone Dorothy's age was always preferable if possible. 'That's good, isn't it?'

'No. I want to see this surgeon. This Jack Armstrong.' The gaze from Dorothy's faded blue eyes was disconcertingly intense. 'I want to see him as soon as possible.'

CHAPTER FIVE

THE ringing of the phone had a muted, dreamlike quality.

Amanda only half roused, to find she was still exactly where she wanted to be, curled within the curve of Jack's arm. Blissfully, she snuggled down again, her cheek enjoying the coarse texture of the dark curls on his chest. Then her eyes opened properly. The ringing hadn't gone away. It didn't sound odd because it was part of a dream. It was...

'Jack, wake up! Your cellphone's ringing.'

The bed dipped and Amanda rolled away as Jack sat up smartly. 'God, I didn't even hear it.'

'It's very quiet. I thought I was dreaming. Where is it?'

'Damned if I know.' Jack was groping around the side of the bed. Amanda clicked on the bedside lamp.

'Where did you leave it?'

'In my jacket. God, woman, there are clothes all over the house.' He picked up a pair of lacy knickers that had somehow ended up hanging from the door-knob. Amanda giggled.

'It wasn't me that threw that particular item.'

'Oh, hell!' Jack muttered. 'It must be the hospital.'

Amanda eyed his naked figure appreciatively. 'It's stopped. Come back to bed.'

Jack stood still. He shook his head and sighed

melodramatically. 'Has anybody ever told you you're insatiable?'

'Never,' Amanda replied honestly. Then she grinned wickedly. 'Am I? Really?'

'Yes.' Jack grinned back. 'Not that I'm complaining, you understand? At least, not yet.'

'No. I hadn't noticed any great aversion on your part. It was you that started it. If you hadn't kissed me like that at the barn dance then I would have kept myself very well under control.'

'It was you that kissed me as I remember it. Anyway, you've had two weeks to get over the novelty. As I see it, the more you get, the more you want.'

'Mmm.' Amanda sat up, hugging her knees. 'As I suggested—come back to bed.'

Jack took two steps towards her and then they both heard the phone begin to ring for the second time. Jack turned and left the room but he was back almost immediately.

'Car accident,' he said tersely. 'One chap with pretty serious injuries. Have you seen my jeans?'

'Try the kitchen.' Amanda checked the clock. Nearly 2 a.m. 'Do you want me?'

Jack's head appeared briefly in the doorway. 'Damned right I do.'

'I meant at the hospital.'

'So did I!' Articles of Amanda's clothing were thrown in the door. A T-shirt landed over Ralph who hadn't moved from his basket in the corner of the room and was looking offended at the night time disturbance. Jack appeared again, fully dressed. 'What else could I have meant, anyway?'

'Ask me later,' Amanda retorted. She stroked Ralph's head gently as she picked up her T-shirt. 'Go back to sleep, old man. Now, where are my shoes?'

It took only minutes for them to arrive in the hospital's emergency department, having run, hand in hand, through the damp stretch of hospital gardens.

'We've got three casualties. It's the driver I've been really worried about but this one's just started to go off.' The registrar on duty stood back a little from the bed. 'He was conscious when he came in but not coherent. Even drunker than the driver, I reckon. His BP's falling steadily. I think he's bleeding heavily but I can't see where. I've only just got an IV line in—we've got a head injury next door.'

Jack had a stethoscope in his ears. He listened to the young man's chest, first one side, then the other. Amanda cut away the remnants of his shirt.

'No breath sounds right side,' Jack told her. He palpated the chest gently. 'I can't feel any broken ribs.'

'There's bruising here, look.' Amanda lifted the now unconscious patient's arm. 'Right in his armpit.'

'He's getting blue,' the registrar warned.

'That's because he's suffocating,' Jack said calmly. 'Mandy, find me a large-bore angiocath.' He took the gloves she held out and put them on as she ripped open more sterile packages.

'He's got a broken rib, concealed by his armpit. Just enough to give him a tiny tear in the lung. More than enough to cause a tension pneumothorax. Scalpel, thanks, Mandy.'

Loud shouts from the next room were followed by

the call of the only nurse on duty in the department. The registrar made a hasty exit.

Jack confidently explored his small incision with a gloved finger. Amanda saw his look of concentration as he inserted the hollow tube. She listened with the stethoscope and nodded at Jack with satisfaction when the breath sounds returned. Jack secured the tube with a suture and Amanda reached for a dressing. The patient's colour was returning rapidly, his BP rising.

'Keep an eye on him, Amanda. And see if you can get a chest X-ray. I'm going to see what's happening next door.'

The young registrar looked relieved to see Jack.

'What's the GCS?'

'It was 14. He was initially very hostile and uncooperative but he's quietened down now and we've managed to get a couple of sutures into this scalp laceration to control haemorrhage.'

Jack looked at the teenager. He was certainly lying quietly enough now, his eyes closed. It was not the best progression of events for a head injury case. 'Any other injuries?'

'Plenty. Broken ribs, arm, right femur. Breathing's OK but he's got an obvious depressed skull fracture under this laceration.'

The cervical collar the boy was wearing was soaked in blood. Jack glanced up at the monitors again. Blood pressure was 85 over 45 and the oxygen saturation 85 per cent.

'Let's get another IV line in. Large bore. I don't want him getting any more hypovolaemic or cardiac output and cerebral perfusion will be compromised.

We need to keep an eye on the oxygen saturation as well. Hypoxia will increase the intracranial pressure. They're both common causes of secondary brain injury.'

The registrar nodded as he swabbed a patch of skin ready for another venepuncture.

'Any CSF from nose or ears?'

'No, but he came in with quite a heavy nosebleed.'

'What's his name?'

'Richard.'

Jack touched the boy's cheek. He spoke loudly. 'Richard? Open your eyes for me.' He clicked on his torch, checking pupil sizes and reactions as the boy complied. 'Do you know where you are?'

The only response was a grunt and an incomprehensible mumble of words. His eyes closed again.

'Open your eyes again, Richard,' Jack called. He laid his hand on the teenager's abdomen. 'Tell me if this hurts.'

This time the response was only a groan. Richard's eyes remained closed. Jack stepped back. 'GCS is dropping,' he stated. 'I'd put it at 11 now. He needs an immediate CT scan. Oxygen saturation is dropping as well.'

Amanda's head appeared around the curtain. 'Do you want me to call Robert Bayliss? He brought the boys in so he won't be far away. I imagine he's waited in case anyone needs transfer to Christchurch.'

Jack nodded. 'We'll have to secure his airway and keep him oxygenated. He should be stable enough to travel within twenty minutes. Someone will have to go with him.'

The registrar looked up from the recordings he was

making on the chart. 'I will,' he offered eagerly. Then
he gave an embarrassed grin. 'My girlfriend's on in
Emergency in Christchurch. Might give me a chance
to say hello.'

'Far be it from me to stand in the way of true love,'
Jack declared. 'Right. Let's get on with sorting out
this airway.'

A few experimental bird calls heralded the approach
of dawn. The cold air was welcome after the heat and
tension of the emergency. Amanda and Jack walked
slowly back towards her flat. Jack took a deep breath.

'You don't get air like this in London.' He looked
up at the still-dark sky. 'And the stars never twinkle.'

Amanda bit her lip. 'I expect you'll miss it,' she
said quietly. 'For a while, anyway.'

Jack pulled her to a halt. 'It's not the stars I'll
miss,' he said abruptly. 'It's you.'

Amanda's lips met his eagerly. For a long moment
they kissed and held each other but the usual spiral
into passion didn't eventuate. Jack pulled back and
looked at Amanda. His dark blue eyes looked almost
black in this light. And they looked more serious than
Amanda had ever seen them.

'I love you, Amanda Morrison.' His gaze was
searching. 'I want you to know that I've never said
that before. Not to anyone. Ever.'

'Oh, Jack,' Amanda breathed. Her first thought was
how sad it must be to live for thirty-six years and
never love anyone enough to tell them. Then the thrill
of his words hit home and she reached up to touch
his face softly. 'I love you, too, Jack.'

'Do you trust me, Mandy? Enough to leave all this

behind? To make a new start?' His hands were gripping her shoulders tensely. 'Do you trust me enough to marry me?'

Amanda hesitated. A new start. A way to leave the past and finally move on. And to do it in the company of someone she loved very deeply. Despite what Dorothy had said, Amanda had no wish to incorporate her past into her future. This could be the perfect solution. But it would mean leaving a lot behind. Some things that had been very precious for a very long time.

'There's nothing for me here,' Jack said, guessing at the reason for her hesitation. 'Nothing but a tie to a past that I can't reconcile myself to. I need to escape. But I want you to come with me. I know it's a big ask. You have ties here.'

Amanda nodded. 'You don't know me that well, Jack. There *are* ties… Like Ralph,' she added quickly.

Jack nodded. 'Maybe I'm asking too much. Too soon. I just wanted you to know how I felt.' He bent and kissed her softly. 'Think about it. I'd better get home and find a change of clothes. Don't forget about that dinner you promised to cook for me tonight.'

Think about it! What chance did she have to think about anything else? Amanda showered and got dressed in her uniform. Ralph was still in his basket and Amanda had to coax him out into the garden.

'Broken nights aren't great, are they?' she sympathised. She left his breakfast biscuits beside his waterbowl and fluffed up the rug that softened the shed doorway and caught the sun by midmorning. 'I'll bring you home a nice bone,' she promised. 'With lots of meaty bits.'

Ralph waved his magnificently feathered tail and Amanda stooped to plant a kiss on the sleek, black head. How could she even contemplate leaving him?

Did she trust Jack Armstrong enough to contemplate marriage? Amanda knew she hadn't been in a position to question that sort of trust the last time she had been in a relationship but that had been years ago. And that relationship had grown slowly out of the friendship she had established with the local veterinarian, Graham Baker. He had become more than a good friend and had wanted to marry her but it had been easy to know that she wasn't ready to trust him on a level deep enough for that sort of commitment. Now the question was less easy to answer and even more of a worry. Trust was too easily betrayed, especially by men.

She had willingly given her trust to Sean, the older student she had met at a dance class in her home town of Dunedin. She had confidently anticipated his support when the accidental pregnancy had become apparent. He had assured her that he was there for her and that they would see it through together. They would get married and live happily ever after. And then he had simply vanished without trace. Moved on, with no forwarding address.

Her trust in her father had been unquestionable. Unshakable and unbelievably shattered by his refusal to have her living under the same roof after what she'd done, or even to speak to her again during the terrible weeks before she'd been packed off to live with her grandmother in Ashburton.

When the baby had come it had been obvious there'd been something wrong. The tiny, pathetic cries of pain had torn through Amanda. She had felt an overwhelming need to comfort and protect the tiny life. But all she'd been able to do had been to put her trust in the doctor who'd happened to be available at the time. And he hadn't even tried...

It had taken years to recover enough confidence to even start another relationship with a man but Graham had been easygoing and gentle. He'd been patient when their relationship had stalled and it had been Amanda who had encouraged him to look elsewhere for the long-term commitment he'd wanted. She hadn't wanted marriage. She hadn't even wanted the promise of it. She hadn't wanted anything that could be so painfully broken. They had drifted apart amicably and Graham had joked that he could never compete in her affections with Ralph, but Amanda had been unhappily aware of the truth beneath the humour. The depth of loyalty, trust and commitment she shared with the dog had been more than she could ever expect from a man.

And here she was again. Busily putting stitches in her life picture that overran the borders she thought she had made secure. Could she keep going? Fill the rest of her life picture with Jack Armstrong woven into the fabric? Amanda managed to shelve her preoccupation long enough to do her usual tour of the wards. The staff change-over had been smooth and everyone was now busy with patient breakfasts, drug rounds and ablutions. The young boy with the pneumothorax from last night was happily attacking the bacon and hash browns Mrs Golder had provided on the menu.

Amanda made a point of going to see Dorothy. Her initial concerns that the media interest would be too much for her old friend were resurfacing. Since the broadcast of the first interviews the hospital had been flooded with requests for further coverage.

Something about the idea of someone celebrating their centenary in a small town and a small country had captured the international imagination. To have lived a hundred years was a remarkable feat in itself. To mark the occasion on the dawn of a new century was a great coincidence. To mark it on the dawn of a new millennium was an opportunity not to be missed.

Kevin Farrow was revelling in the attention, managing to push his own agenda regarding the vital function of a full medical service in a rural area. Local hotels and businesses were also delighted as a stream of visitors steadily increased. Dorothy McFadden might have only intended to visit Ashburton but she had been claimed firmly as one of their own. A remarkable woman who now symbolised the departing century.

Dorothy's philosophy had also been adopted as a millennium theme. The television programme had been titled *Stitches in Time* and people were eager to know more about the tapestry of Dorothy's life and to tell her of their own. Cards and letters for her overloaded the hospital mail system. Perhaps that was why Dorothy hadn't touched her needlework for days now. She insisted on going through the mail each day herself, impatiently opening letters with the aid of an old ivory letter-opener grasped in a shaking hand. Amanda had the impression that she was expecting something in particular but the aura of disappointment when each session finished was easily explained by an obvious weariness.

This morning Amanda was surprised to find Dorothy still in her bed, her hair unbrushed. 'It's not like you to sleep in, Dorothy. Are you feeling all right?'

'I'm fine. Stop fussing, Amanda.'

Amanda's step slowed. The tetchy tone was also unusual and Dorothy's cheeks looked a little flushed. 'I can cancel the people coming to see you today if you don't feel up to another interview.'

'Who's coming?' The stare was intense. The faded eyes glittered oddly and Amanda felt a twinge of alarm.

'It's only people from the local paper today. They want to hear your memories of Ashburton during the war years.'

'Oh. Do people read it? This local paper?'

'I believe so.' Amanda smiled. 'It's got a lot of farming and rugby news in it as well.'

'More people than watch the television?'

'No. It would only be read by people living in Ashburton, I expect.'

'Will they write to me?' Dorothy sounded querulous and Amanda felt another twinge of concern. Dorothy pulled at her bedcovers. 'Help me up, Nurse. I've got to get dressed.'

'They're not coming until later this afternoon. Why don't you stay in bed and rest?'

'No. I must think. I can't think in bed. What will I say, Amanda? How much should I tell him?'

'No more than you want to. You don't have to talk to them at all.'

'Oh, but I do. There's not enough time. I need to tell him.' Dorothy looked around her, agitated. 'How else is he going to know?' Her gaze fastened on Amanda again. 'Or do you think it's better if he doesn't know?'

She was confused. A perfectly acceptable state of mind for a ninety-nine-year-old but Amanda intended to sit in on today's interview. She was also going to get Colin Garrett to give Dorothy a thorough check-up. Her instincts told her that something wasn't right.

It was a day for meetings. Housekeeping, supply and purchasing, touching base with the home support staff and a planning session for a staff development programme. Amanda had information on courses available in all the main centres for the coming year, along with requests from interested nursing staff members. The prospect of trying to make recommendations was too much for her after losing a night's sleep.

The mid-afternoon staff change-over gave her an excuse to leave her office and check on ward developments and then it was time for Dorothy's interview. Relieved to find the old woman looking alert and sounding quite coherent, Amanda relaxed a little and was quickly lost in fascination at some of Dorothy's information.

'You're not going to believe this!'

Jack Armstrong paused as he twisted the corkscrew

he was holding. He looked up expectantly.

'You know Dorothy McFadden? Our ninety-nine-year-old?'

'How could I not? I'm expecting her photo to go up on the whiteboard in the foyer. You know, 23 days to go. Dorothy McFadden welcomes the new millennium.' He eased the cork from the bottle. 'Didn't you say something about me having a look at an ulcer on her foot?'

'Yes, but things are improving. We bumped up the physiotherapy and it seems to have had a positive effect on blood supply and healing. Colin Garrett doesn't think she'll need a skin graft after all.'

Jack nodded. 'Good.' Then his face twisted into a grimace. 'Now all I need to do is work a miracle with Mrs Golder's bunions. We've booked her in for late January.'

Amanda laughed. 'Never mind Mrs Golder. Do you know where Dorothy McFadden worked when she came out to New Zealand in 1916?'

'In Ashburton.'

'Yes, but specifically.'

'How did she get out here in the middle of a war?'

'She got passage on a ship that came out to collect troops. But that's not what I found really fascinating. She worked for your family, Jack. She was a servant at Ashcroft.'

Jack handed her the glass of wine. 'That would have been in the time of my grandfather. John Arthur the second. Or was it the third? He was too old to go to the war—in his forties. My father was born in 1918.'

'Yes. That's what Dorothy said. She said she left the day the present owner of Ashcroft was born. The fourth of August 1918. She made quite a point about remembering the exact date.'

'Long-term memory in the elderly is often far more accurate than short-term.'

'That makes your father quite old.'

'Just turned eighty-one. Let's see, I'm thirty-six. That means he would have been forty-five when I was born.'

'Is that a family tradition. To have children so late?'

Jack shrugged. 'I've avoided assimilating any family traditions. My mother shattered the mould by deserting. They belong in the past along with that museum of a house. You should see some of the ancient furniture collecting dust.'

'I'd love to,' Amanda said eagerly.

'What?' Jack sounded surprised.

'The house has always fascinated me,' Amanda confessed. 'There's something about it. An air of mystery. Hearing Dorothy talk today, I could imagine it teeming with servants and getting ready for the annual ball your family held. It seems asleep now.'

'Not asleep. Dead,' Jack said shortly. 'With a non-resuscitation order slapped on it.' He caught Amanda's eye. 'You can see it if you really want to. I'll give you the grand tour.'

'When? Won't your father mind?'

'I doubt he'd even notice. The GP's increased his morphia now. He's sleeping a lot of the time. What about Saturday?'

*   *   *

It was like stepping back in time, turning through the gates and driving between the grand old trees onto the circular carriage drive. The huge front door stood slightly ajar and Amanda was almost surprised to find it swung open by Jack and not a uniformed butler.

'Welcome to Ashcroft,' he said solemnly. Amanda was aware of the tension in his lips as he kissed her and she wondered if she had made a mistake in requesting the invitation. Or perhaps his father had disturbed him. Amanda shivered suddenly and Jack's glance was quick.

'It's freezing in here even in midsummer. That's why they made it so big. You could keep warm with all the exercise of moving from one room to another.'

Amanda gazed around the entrance to the stately home. The walls were half covered in wood panelling. To her right, the area widened into a seating area of leather couches grouped in front of a cavernous open fireplace. She could imagine a fire going, the glow reflected in the golden tones of the wood and the rich red of the ancient Persian-style carpeting, glinting in the facets of the impressive chandelier they stood beneath. Now the cold-blackened hole only added to a feeling that this house had not been really lived in for a very long time.

Ahead of Amanda a wide staircase with an intricately carved banister curved gracefully upwards. Her eye followed its invitation and she was stunned by the stained-glass window that marked the landing where the staircase began a return curve.

'Come on.' Jack was already moving up the stairs. 'We'll do the formal areas later.'

Amanda paused on the landing, admiring the deep

colours of the window. A shield was depicted in the centre, the name 'Armstrong' etched into the glass.

'This house was built for your ancestor, wasn't it?' Amanda was overwhelmed by the sense of how much Jack Armstrong belonged here. 'No one else has ever owned the house?'

'Until now,' Jack muttered. 'Over a hundred years and I'll be the one who has to hand it over.'

'The name will always be there.' Amanda was still gazing at the window.

'Not for long, I wouldn't think. Who could afford to do what this place needs? Especially without the income from the farm. The roof leaks, the wiring needs attention, the bathrooms are virtually useless!'

'They said in the paper that there's an historical protection listing. Nobody will be allowed to pull it down.'

'They won't have to. It'll just crumble.' Jack moved ahead. 'We've got all the main bedrooms on this floor. There's about ten of them but let's start in the servants' quarters. That's where your Miss McFadden would have lived.'

'She said she had an attic room, above the main quarters.'

The tour took more than an hour and Jack's enthusiasm grew. Amanda was enchanted with the warren of plain rooms for the servants, with the small staircase down into the kitchens and service areas. She loved the round bedrooms that formed parts of the turrets and was awestruck by the sheer size of the ballroom that extended along the whole south side of the ground floor.

'There's got to be some way to save this house,' she told Jack passionately. 'There's just got to be.'

'I had the same thought myself,' Jack admitted. 'I walked back in here and all those early memories came flooding back. The feeling of being part of the place was even stronger than the memories. I was filled with a passionate ambition to save it all. I think my father recognised my reaction. It must have been his ace to try and make me leave again—telling me that an outfit called Starbright International Limited now owned it all and there was nothing here for me.'

Amanda was disturbed by Jack's bitter tone. Hoping to distract him, she turned away from the pretty drawing room at the base of one of the turrets and moved quickly towards the matching door at the base of the other turret. 'What's in here? Another drawing room?'

'Don't go in there,' Jack warned. But it was too late. Amanda had already opened the door and ducked through.

An elderly man was sitting in an armchair, his feet propped on a leather footstool, a rug over his knees. The room was a library, judging by the floor-to-ceiling shelves full of books that bordered two walls, but it had been converted into a bedsitting room. A tray on a table was cluttered with drug containers. An oxygen cylinder and mask stood beside the bed.

'Who are you?' The man looked startled by the intrusion but the anger set in instantly. 'I've told you, I'm not having any damned reporters snooping around this house. Get out!'

Jack's arm went around Amanda. 'This is Amanda

Morrison, Dad. She's a friend of mine. She works at the hospital.'

'Well, get her out. It's all their fault we're being pestered now. Just because some geriatric ex-servant decides to have her birthday here.' John Armstrong coughed painfully. The coughing worsened and Amanda could hear the struggle for breath. Automatically she moved, reaching for the glass of water and holding it for Jack's father to sip from as the coughing subsided. He pushed the glass away irritably. Jack had also moved, picking up the oxygen cylinder and placing it beside his father's chair.

John Armstrong glared at Amanda. 'I know you, don't I?'

'I don't think so, Mr Armstrong.'

'*Dr* Armstrong. Are you a nurse?'

'Yes.'

'That's where I've seen you, then. At the hospital.' John Armstrong's voice was weak. He was still gasping for breath. Jack held out the oxygen mask.

'Let me put this on, Dad.'

'Leave me alone. Get Mrs Bennett and then leave me alone.'

Jack's hand hovered as his father took a deep, rasping breath. 'There's nothing you can do to change anything. Get out and let nature take its course.' He coughed and then drew another slow, ragged breath. 'It's all for the best anyway.' John closed his eyes and lay back in his chair.

Jack's mouth tightened. He put the mask on his father's lap. 'I'll go and call Mrs Bennett. Come with me, Amanda.'

But Amanda didn't move. She was standing at the

foot of the chair, her eyes riveted on his father, an expression of horror on her face. Suddenly Jack felt a wave of anger. He had known this was a bad idea. Traipsing around this house, reliving childhood memories and allowing the hold the past had on him to gather new strength. He was angry at his father for forcing him away from the roots he'd had here. Angry that his father was dying and didn't care about the wreckage he was leaving behind.

And he was angry at Amanda for seeing his father like this and—worse—for looking as though he were some sort of monster from the deep. She had seen terminally ill patients before, hadn't she? Ignoring her, Jack marched out of the room.

Amanda tried to move but her feet weren't ready to obey her. John Armstrong *had* seen her at the hospital. Only once. She had never known his name, would never have recognised him without some sort of prompt. He had simply been a doctor, called in because, for some reason, nobody else in the hospital had been available at the time. It had been his words that had triggered the memory. And through the words came the recognition of the voice and the man he had been ten years ago.

The man who had looked at the face and body of her newborn child. The man who had touched the baby Amanda hadn't been allowed to hold. The man who had said, 'There's nothing any of us can do that's going to change the outcome. Take her away and let nature take its course.' And then he had looked at Amanda, still in pain, still frightened and still so very alone. 'You're not married, are you, Miss Morrison?'

he had stated calmly. 'Well, it's probably all for the best, then, isn't it?'

The man whom Amanda had hated. His callous words had haunted her, his instructions to remove her baby only deepening the emotional pain Amanda had dealt with through the years. One of the few direct links to a past she had hoped to escape. The father of the man with whom the escape had seemed possible. Now Jack was tied to her own past. And she still wanted to escape. Amanda stumbled in her haste to get out of the room. Away from this man. Away from this house. Away from Jack.

Jack was on the other side of the door, the house-keeper following him. He caught her arm. 'What's wrong, Amanda?'

She twisted free, moving aside to let the house-keeper past. Jack was staring at her.

'Why are you so upset? Did my father say something to you?'

'Yes… No.' Amanda shook her head. 'I have to go, Jack.'

'I'll come with you.'

'No!' Amanda's tone was unintentionally horrified. Jack took a step back.

'I'm sorry if he upset you,' Jack said stiffly. 'But he does have a point. There've been a lot of people turning up since that newspaper article. My father's kept to himself for a long time and he's in no condition to handle public scrutiny now.'

Amanda took the conversational escape route eagerly. 'Maybe it's a good thing. The more interest there is in the house the more possibility that it could be saved.'

'What, as some sort of tourist attraction?' Jack said in disgust.

'If that's what it takes. It's a piece of history, Jack. And a beautiful house. It's worth preserving at any cost.'

'It's cost too much already,' Jack said angrily. 'And I'm the one who's paying.'

'Perhaps you need to look at it from a less selfish point of view.'

'Selfish!' Now Jack looked really angry. The flop of dark hair had come right down over his forehead.

'There are a lot of people who have been associated with this property,' Amanda said doggedly. 'It's part of a community. It doesn't exist in isolation.'

'It would be better if it didn't exist at all,' Jack snapped. 'I should never have come back. I should never have brought you here.'

'No,' Amanda agreed slowly. 'I shouldn't have come. You can't escape your past, Jack. And I can't escape mine. Dorothy's right. You can't start a new scene in isolation. It would leave too big a gap.'

'What the hell are you talking about?' Jack pushed his hair back off his forehead forcefully, narrowing his eyes as he glared at Amanda.

She edged down the steps. 'This. Me—us. It won't work, Jack. It can't possibly work.'

'You're *dumping* me?' Jack's face was as incredulous as his tone. 'Because my *father* said something to upset you?'

'It's more than that—'

'I can see that.' Jack's response was viciously swift. Amanda could see the pain in his eyes and hated herself for causing it. 'Well, don't let me stop you walking out, Amanda. It all seems terribly appropriate somehow. This family is destined to be destroyed. Along with their precious house. You'll be better off without me.'

'Jack, wait!' Amanda took a step up but she was too late. The enormous front door closed in her face with an unnerving finality. She felt fear grip her. The hope she had allowed herself of a future that could undo the past had been given a mortal blow. The emptiness she felt replacing it filled her with dread. Then anger bubbled up through the fear and took command. Jack had shown himself to be made of the same stuff as all the men in her life. If the going got tough they simply walked away.

He was right, Amanda decided, wrenching open her car door. She *would* be better off without him.

CHAPTER SIX

THE sense of foreboding wouldn't go away.

Perhaps it was simply the aftermath of the scene with Jack and the break-up of their relationship. It wasn't easy to avoid contact at the hospital and the last few days had been miserable. It could have been so different, too. Jack had approached her first thing on Monday morning. His smile had been one of relief.

'You did me a favour, Amanda.'

'Sorry?' Amanda's heart had beaten with painful irregularity. Was he going to tell her he hadn't wanted the relationship anyway and was glad to be free of her?

'I was so angry after you left. I demanded that my father tell me what he had done to upset you so much.'

Amanda felt a sudden chill. Could John Armstrong have remembered her? Remembered the cruelty with which he had treated her and her baby? 'What did he tell you?' she whispered.

'He denied it. We argued. In fact, we had a blazing row and said things I never thought could be said on either side. I told him I hated him and what he'd done to the family. What he'd done to the house and especially what he'd done to me.'

'I'm surprised he had the strength,' Amanda said quietly. She wasn't sure whether she felt relieved or not. Would it make any difference if Jack knew the truth? Yes, her mind shouted at her. It would make all the difference. They could repair the damage. Jack could understand why she hated his father—he shared that feeling.

'I was surprised, too,' Jack nodded. 'But what surprised me more was what came later. He called me back. It was nearly midnight. I almost didn't go. I had packed my bags and was ready to leave for good.'

'And?'

Jack was looking somewhere over Amanda's shoulder. He spoke softly. 'We talked. For the first time in my life we really *talked*. He told me things about himself I'd never even guessed at. He kept going despite being in pain and totally exhausted. He didn't stop until 6 o'clock this morning and by then I actually felt I knew my father.' Jack's gaze locked with Amanda's. 'I got to know my Dad, Amanda. I could forgive him. I could even admire him.'

Amanda swallowed. They were not sentiments she could ever share.

'I suppose that was why I came in the first place,' Jack continued. 'I didn't want my father to die with me hating him. I wanted to understand why things had gone so wrong. Why I was going to be denied the family heritage.' He took hold of Amanda's hand.

'It's you I have to thank for this. I had given up any hope of sorting it out. I was ready to give up and take you away. Escape from it all and start again. But we don't have to. We could stay here and build a life together. Maybe there's even some way we could buy Ashcroft back. Would you like that? Shall we start a new generation of Armstrongs and bring Ashcroft back to life?'

Amanda's head was shaking as she tried to deny the pain and confusion Jack's words evoked. She tried to withdraw her hand but Jack held it tightly. 'What's the matter, Mandy? Don't you see? This changes everything.'

It did change everything. It changed the hope that Jack might understand the pain of her loss and the blame she had laid at his father's feet. Jack had come here an angry man, his life poisoned by his past and his relationship with his father. He had found peace and Amanda could see just how much it meant to him. How could she now confess her own feelings and destroy the achievement he had thought beyond reach? Amanda struggled to find something to say. Suddenly the pressure on her hand was gone.

'Perhaps it doesn't change anything.' The warmth in Jack's eyes had vanished. The stare was almost calculating. 'I can see you're not exactly over the moon at the prospect of a future with me.'

'I'm sorry, Jack. I…' Again, Amanda was lost for words. She wanted to ask for time. Time to arrange her thoughts and feelings to try and find some way around the emotional obstacle she had to contend with. But Jack took her apology to be for something quite different.

'So that's it, then? No, thanks, but *sorry*?'

Amanda opened her mouth to speak but Jack cut her off angrily. 'I don't want your apology, Amanda. I don't want you feeling sorry for me. Forget it. Forget the whole bloody thing.'

Amanda didn't see him walk away. She had her eyes clenched as tightly as her fists.

* * *

Surely that was the worst thing that could have happened. So why did the sense that worse was to come haunt Amanda now?

Perhaps it was because Ralph seemed suddenly much older. He had been reluctant to leave his basket in the mornings ever since that night she and Jack had been called in to deal with the car accident victims. Now his breakfast biscuits had been left uneaten for the last two days. If he didn't seem brighter tonight she would have to take him to see Graham.

Amanda could see the old dog now as she stood on Ward 2's verandah. He lay, sleeping, on his rug in the sun. A still shape. Very still. The sense of dread suddenly sharpened and Amanda's heart skipped a beat but then she saw Ralph stand up, stretch and turn around twice, before settling onto his rug again. Amanda breathed a sigh of relief and felt irritated by her own fear. There were more important things she had to worry about right now.

Like Dorothy McFadden. Their celebrity patient had started running a mild temperature after the weekend and by yesterday had developed a dry cough, joint pains and headache. Amanda had cancelled all visits and was worried by Dorothy's lack of appetite and interest in her surroundings. Kevin Farrow was even more worried when he'd heard of the development yesterday.

'It must be this flu. That can be a killer for somebody Dorothy's age. We've got to do something, Amanda.'

'We're doing everything we can. Dorothy was vaccinated for flu. It's probably just a mild virus that she'll shake off.'

'God, I hope so. It's only sixteen days till New Year. We're going to have to have a full-scale press conference on the day to accommodate everyone who wants to see Dorothy on her birthday. You'll have to take special care of her.'

'I will, anyway.' Amanda had been annoyed at the inference that Dorothy's special status made her condition more serious.

Amanda hurried in from the verandah now, having checked on Ralph. Stopping in Dorothy's room, she was alarmed to find that the old woman's temperature and heart rate had risen quite sharply. Her skin felt hot and dry and her pale eyes glittered feverishly. Amanda sponged her with a soft lukewarm cloth, having put out an urgent call to Colin Garrett. He examined Dorothy gently, his manner cheerful, but his face was concerned when he beckoned Amanda out of the room.

'It could be the start of pneumonia. Her chest is dull to percussion with bronchial breath sounds over the left lower zone.' Colin folded his stethoscope and pushed it back into his white coat pocket. 'We'll get some bloods off and take a chest X-ray but I think we'll start some IV antibiotics immediately. It might be a good idea to move her to Intensive Care. We'll need to keep a close eye on her respiratory and cardiac function. Have you talked to her at all about intensive nursing or resuscitation preferences?'

Amanda took a deep breath. Kevin would have a fit if he knew of this conversation. 'Not specifically. Dorothy's well aware of her age and the limited time she has left. But she's been astonishingly fit up until now and has hinted quite frequently that she had some unfinished business.'

Colin's eyebrows were raised with curiosity. 'Do you know what it is?'

'No. Some things she keeps quite private. I think it was the reason that brought her back to Ashburton, though. Maybe it has something to do with Ashcroft—where she used to work.' Amanda sighed. How many lives, had been touched by that house and the Armstrong family? she wondered. And did any of them have happy memories of their association?

'Well, we'll do what we can, within reason,' Colin decided. 'Keep a close eye on her and call me if you're worried about anything.'

'I'll do that,' Amanda promised. 'I'm pretty clear of other commitments today. We've got both our mid-wives away at a training course but we don't have any deliveries scheduled for more than a week so I shouldn't have to fill in there.'

She had spoken too soon. Not only did a local farmer's wife, Charlotte Wallace, come in late that afternoon with premature labour but the baby was in trouble. As soon as Amanda saw the slow heart rate on the foetal monitor she knew she had to call in Jack.

'Have you noticed any decrease in the baby's movements in the last day or two?' Jack queried, having talked to Charlotte about the signs of her labour which had started two hours previously.

'It's been less active for a week or so, I guess. I thought it was just getting bigger. Not so much room to move around.'

Jack caught Amanda's eye briefly. At thirty weeks'

gestation the movements should certainly not be restricted.

'Your waters haven't broken and you haven't started dilating yet but I'm not very happy about the baby's condition,' Jack told the parents cautiously. 'We certainly don't want to do anything about stopping the labour if there's anything wrong. We'll run some more tests but we may need to consider a Caesarean even though it's so early.'

Jack did the urgent ultrasound scan himself. 'I'm no expert,' he reported back to Amanda, 'but I have sat in on some teaching sessions in London and I'd say we could be looking at some major cardiac abnormalities.' He kept his voice too low to be overheard. 'The scan suggests an aplastic left ventricle—no real development at all.'

'Then it's not something that could be corrected,' Amanda whispered forlornly. 'Or survived even for a short time.'

'I can't be sure.' Jack shook his head. 'It needs more technical skill than I've got to diagnose accurately. If it is something this major I can't understand why it wasn't picked up much earlier than this.' He crossed the room to speak to Charlotte. 'When did you have your last scan?' he queried.

'I had one at about eight weeks to confirm the pregnancy,' Charlotte said, 'but we missed the one at sixteen weeks. We were supposed to go up to Christchurch for that but we live so far out of town and we were having trouble with the truck.'

'What about antenatal checks?'

'I haven't been in for those either,' Charlotte confessed. 'Things seemed to be going so well until I got this flu.' She looked alarmed. 'Is there something wrong?'

'We think the baby might have some heart problems,' Jack told her gently. 'And the placenta isn't looking too good. I'm not surprised that you've gone into premature labour. I don't think we have any option other than to go ahead with an immediate Caesarean. You're dilating now and I don't think the baby would have much chance of surviving a vaginal delivery.'

Charlotte paled as his words sank in. Amanda moved closer and took hold of her hand. Jack's face was expressionless. 'Could you alert Theatre, please, Amanda? I'll get Tom down to do an epidural. I'll be ready to scrub in twenty minutes.'

Charlotte's grasp on Amanda's hand was painful. 'Stay with me, please, Amanda? In the theatre? Brian won't be able to cope with it and I'm really scared.'

Amanda glanced at Jack but he avoided her eye contact. 'Of course I will,' she promised Charlotte. 'I'll just have to make a quick phone call and check on a patient. I'll be with you before you go up to Theatre.'

The phone call was to the veterinary clinic. 'Graham? I wanted to ask a favour. I'm stuck at the hospital and I'm a bit worried about Ralph. He's not eating well and seems very slowed down. Could you check on him on your way home? There's a spare key under his water bowl. Let him in, will you? I don't want him getting cold.'

'I'm heading off now, Mandy. Don't worry. I'll look after our boy.'

The visit was to Dorothy McFadden. Now running

a high temperature and respiration rate, the old woman was, for the moment, asleep. ECG electrodes had been attached to the papery skin. The monitor showed a rapid trace. One arm had been splinted to protect the IV line now administering the antibiotics they hoped would control the infection. The blood tests had confirmed the impression given by the examination and the opaque area in the left lung on Dorothy's chest X-ray that they were, indeed, dealing with pneumonia. The oxygen saturation monitor clipped to her finger showed a reading of just under ninety per cent despite the oxygen being delivered by nasal cannulae. Dorothy's breathing sounded stressed.

Amanda pulled the curtains closed again behind her. It didn't look good. Pneumonia might be a welcome visitor to some very elderly and unwell people but Dorothy wasn't ready to die. If it was inevitable, however, Amanda was determined that her friend would not die alone. She told Colin Garrett that she would return as soon as she could and would stay with Dorothy overnight.

Theatre was the last place Amanda wanted to be. She was worried about Ralph. Graham had phoned to say he was going to take the dog home with him overnight and wanted to run some tests in the morning. 'He's got some abdominal pain,' he had told Amanda. 'I'd like to do a scan and check things out thoroughly.'

She was worried about Dorothy. The whole community was excited by the prospect of her birthday and the attention the town would receive on New Year's Day. The street party planned for New Year's

Eve had been renamed 'Dorothy's Birthday Bash' in honour of their new celebrity. They were planning to present her with the key to the town, were talking about renaming one of the larger parks after her and wanted to grant any wish that might persuade her to spend the rest of her days here. A lot of people would be devastated by her death at this point but none more so than Amanda. Dorothy had become like family, a replacement for her much-loved grandmother.

She also didn't want to be in Theatre because Jack was the surgeon. There was too much emotional involvement. Memories of passion, hope created and destroyed. Anger. Unfinished business that generated an unbearable tension. It could be put aside in a professional situation. They were both too experienced to let it affect their work. But even a background personal tension could remove any enjoyment or satisfaction in even a successful outcome.

And the likelihood of a successful outcome here was distressingly remote. It was all far too close to home for Amanda. Charlotte had been given an epidural. Her husband Brian, a shy young farmer, had indeed been totally overwhelmed by the high-tech atmosphere and couldn't cope with the idea of witnessing the surgery. There was no point in trying to persuade him. His own distress would be of no support to his wife. It was left to Amanda to hold the young mother's hand, calm her fears and talk with enough reassurance and comfort to help her through a very traumatic experience.

Colin Garrett was present, in the hope that his paediatric skills could be needed for a resuscitation of the baby. A portable incubator was in the theatre.

Robert Bayliss was standing by with an ambulance for a potential dash to the specialist neonatal ICU in Christchurch.

Unfortunately, Robert wasn't called on for an emergency dash. From the moment the baby boy left Jack's hands only minutes after the initial incision and the umbilical cord was severed it was clear that there was no chance. It took only minutes for the tiny heart to give up any attempt at beating. Colin worked on, intubating and ventilating the baby, his face grim and distressed as he administered drugs that could potentially stimulate some cardiac response. Jack continued with the much longer phase of the surgery, painstakingly tidying up and closing the wound. Charlotte couldn't fail to sense the despair in the room. Her face was distraught.

'Look after him for me, please, Amanda?'

There was nothing medical Amanda could do. There was nothing any of them could do. Colin left quietly some time later and Amanda spent her time gently cleaning the baby, removing the intubation tube and IV line and wrapping the already chilled body in a soft linen sheet.

Charlotte turned her head enough to see Amanda at this point. She burst into anguished sobs. 'He's dead, isn't he?' she cried.

Jack motioned for Amanda to leave as Tom and the theatre staff tried to comfort Charlotte. Amanda hesitated. How could she simply remove the baby before Charlotte had even seen him? Jack's expression was furious at her delay. He jerked his head towards the door and his tone was dismissive. 'Thank you, Nurse. We can manage without you now.'

'Charlotte?' Amanda stepped closer to the sobbing woman. 'Do you want me to take your baby away?'

Charlotte's eyes were screwed tightly shut. She looked terrified. 'Yes,' she sobbed. 'I don't want to see it.' Her voice rose hysterically. *'Take it away!'*

'Now, Nurse!' Jack ground out between his teeth. His glare was accusing and Amanda knew she had no choice. Miserably, she turned and left the theatre.

It was perhaps the hardest thing Amanda had ever done, carrying the tiny bundle to the cold, clinical surroundings of the mortuary. Surprisingly, it was the first time she had ever held a dead baby. Or perhaps not surprisingly as it was a situation she had automatically done her best to avoid.

So this is what it would have felt like. It looked as though she carried a doll. A tiny porcelain face—the perfect portrait of a sleeping infant, folds of soft fabric gently draping the tiny features. There was reality in the touch. A reality Amanda had never had the opportunity to experience. This baby could be touched, spoken to, loved and grieved over. Amanda was unaware of the tears streaming down her face as she walked through a deserted and darkened hospital. Deep within her she knew it was her own child she grieved for. The touch and finality of what she held in her arms had released a burden she had not been aware of carrying all these years.

An almost peaceful calm settled over Amanda shortly after the sad journey as she took her position beside Dorothy McFadden's bedside. Dorothy was feverishly turning her head from side to side, muttering to herself and restlessly plucking at her bed sheets with her unsplinted hand. Amanda supported the old woman's head as she turned over and rearranged the pillows to provide a cooler surface. She sponged Dorothy's face and as much of her body as she could without disturbing her patient and then adjusted the fan on the bedside table to provide a cooling breeze. Dorothy's eyes opened when Amanda held a stethoscope against her chest to check her breathing. Her respiration rate was now an alarming thirty-two per minute.

'Amanda?' The voice was a croak. 'Are you here?'

'I'm here, Dorothy,' Amanda said soothingly. 'I'm not going anywhere else. I'll be right beside you.' She smoothed a salve onto Dorothy's cracked lips.

'My chest hurts, dear. It's hard to breathe.'

'I know. Try and rest, Dorothy. I'll put this oxygen mask back on for a while.' The oxygen saturation levels had dropped well below ninety per cent so the nasal cannulae had been exchanged for a mask that could deliver a higher concentration of oxygen.

In the early hours of Christmas Eve Dorothy roused, suddenly agitated.

'Where's my baby?' she called hoarsely. 'They've taken my baby away.'

Amanda woke from her exhausted sleep, confused. For a moment she thought it was Charlotte calling. 'I've taken care of him,' she responded quietly. 'I'll bring him to you in the morning.' She moved her body, aware of the painful cramp in her leg, and realised she was curled in an armchair. Horrified, she also realised she was speaking to Dorothy, not Charlotte. But her words had calmed the feverish old woman.

'Thank you,' she gasped. 'I just want to see him.

Just once. I won't make any trouble.' The heavy rattle as Dorothy coughed brought Amanda to her feet.

'Dorothy? Are you all right?' The oxygen mask had been pushed off her face and was caught under her chin.

'I know I promised.' Dorothy was staring at her, unseeing. The dim light gave her eyes an eerie intensity. Amanda reached for her pulse. 'I just want to see him. Just for a minute.'

'Your son?' Amanda asked softly. 'Do you want to see your son, Dorothy?'

'Yes.' The rasping indrawn breath sounded like a sob. 'Just once. *Please.*'

Amanda caught the agitated hand. 'How old are you, Dorothy?'

'I'm eighteen.'

'Where are you?'

'Here, of course. At Ashcroft.' Dorothy drew another difficult breath and her eyes fluttered shut. Alarmed, Amanda reached for her pulse again, her eyes flicking towards the monitor, fully expecting to see an arrhythmia heralding a dramatic decline in her condition. The touch was as reassuring as the screen. The heart rate was still fast but it was there, and steady. Her respiration rate was still over thirty and the oxygen saturation had dropped to eighty-five per cent. As she replaced the mask Dorothy seemed to drop back into a deep sleep. Amanda checked the monitors and the IV line, sponged Dorothy again and sat watching, amazed at what she had learned from the delirious conversation.

No wonder she had felt such an affinity to this woman, with a shared experience such as that. Pieces

of the puzzle fell into place. This must have been why
Dorothy had returned to Ashburton. This was where
she had given birth to her son. A baby that had been
taken away before she'd had the chance to hold him.
Had the baby died? Had Dorothy come to find a grave
site? Or had he been adopted? Was Dorothy searching
for a son who may have spent his life in this area—
may even still be alive? She leaned over to stroke the
wisps of white hair off Dorothy's forehead.

'I'll help you find him,' she whispered. 'We'll do
it together, Dorothy. I know how important it is.'

Dorothy McFadden slept. The sounds she made
could have been snoring. They could also indicate a
further deterioration in her breathing. But the oxygen
saturation hadn't dropped any further and the sounds
were steady. Eventually they lulled Amanda back into
her exhausted doze where images of babies, alive and
dead, tormented her unconscious mind.

She woke just before dawn and was grateful for the
respite from her dreams. For a minute she sat, sa-
vouring the silence. Then a cold prickle of fear swept
over her as she realised why it was so quiet.
Dorothy's loud snores had stopped. She still looked
to be sleeping, her eyes peacefully closed, but the
feverish flush of the soft skin on her cheeks had paled.
Amanda scrambled to her feet. Why hadn't any
alarms on the monitors gone off? How could she have
slept through what she'd promised Dorothy she
wouldn't allow to happen to her alone. Almost before
she had formed the thought, the curtain slid quietly
open.

'Morning, Mandy.' The cheerfully whispered
greeting of the night nurse made Amanda turn swiftly.

'Dorothy,' she said urgently. 'She's…' Amanda couldn't quite say it. Didn't want to believe it.

'She's looking much better, isn't she?' The night nurse smiled with satisfaction. 'The oxygen sats have been going up steadily. I almost woke you up to tell you but you looked so tired.'

'I… I…' Amanda stared at the monitor. In her distress she had managed to block out the screen with its silent cardiac trace and the red numerals recording various measurements, including an oxygen saturation now up to ninety-five per cent and a temperature and respiration rate that was well down. 'I *was* tired,' she said faintly. 'It's been a long night.'

'I'll say.' The nurse checked her watch. 'Only an hour till I go home. I doubt I'll get much sleep, though. You wouldn't believe how much Christmas shopping I've still got to do.'

Amanda smiled and found herself very close to tears. She had a gift at home for Dorothy which she had chosen weeks ago—tiny, gold-plated embroidery scissors in the shape of a stork, with the blades forming the long beak and the finger holes the feet. The matching thimble rested with the scissors in a velvet-lined box. She had been looking forward to presenting Dorothy with the gift. And the opportunity hadn't been taken away.

'If Dorothy wakes up, tell her I'll be back by breakfast-time,' Amanda said. 'I must go home and have a shower and change.'

There was a large Christmas tree in the hospital foyer. The light was still dim enough to make the twinkling lights cast coloured shadows. The whiteboard flashed pink and then blue and green as Amanda walked wearily past.

'8 days to go', the board read. The message was now in a balloon coming from a rather badly drawn but very excited image of Rudolf. 'Merry Christmas' had been added as an afterthought. Christmas celebrations were only a prelude this year. The big event was still a week away. Amanda wasn't bothered by the preoccupation. Celebration of Christmas had never been a priority for her. In fact, for many years she had avoided it as much as possible. Memories she preferred not to resurrect were too closely associated with this time of year. Far from being happy, it was a period Amanda dreaded.

This year could possibly be the hardest one yet. For now, thanks to Jack Armstrong, she could add the recognition of her own loneliness to her list of regrets. And the birth and death of a short-lived dream that had destroyed the contentment of the existence she had created for herself.

But the stitches in time could not be undone.

And things could never be quite the same again.

CHAPTER SEVEN

THE news Amanda received at 10.30 a.m. on Christmas Eve was devastating.

It was a mark of real friendship that he had come to tell her face to face. The warmth of the human contact had softened the blow just a little. Amanda closed her eyes, allowing the warmth of the sun to dry the last traces of her tears but then she moved decisively, turning away from the sanctuary of the hospital gardens to enter the main building. Time alone now could only bring self-recrimination. Agonising over whether her attention had been too self-directed recently and whether a different course of action would have made any difference. It couldn't help now, of course, and could only add to the depth of misery. Distraction was the best means of defence and there was always plenty to be found in her work.

The usual hospital routines went out the window at this time of year. Outpatient clinics were suspended, elective surgery postponed. Any inpatients that could be discharged were sent home to be with their families, and general staff was reduced to a skeleton with others placed on call for emergencies. And yet the bustle only seemed to increase.

Visitors poured through the doors, determined to bring as much seasonal cheer as possible to the people left isolated by their injuries, illness or work commitments. As Amanda entered the foyer she found a local choir organising themselves to tour the wards and sing Christmas carols. One of the more popular bakeries had sent trays of mince pies which were about to be distributed for morning tea. Karen, sporting a reindeer horns headband and a red nose, was sampling a mince pie. One of the paper chains she had attached to the ceiling came adrift at that point, trailing gracefully down to drape itself over the choir members. There was much laughter as they disentangled themselves. Mince pies were offered all around.

Amanda hurried past. She would check on Dorothy again and then shut herself away in her office. She was certainly in no mood to join in the festive atmosphere. She was startled to see Jack at the top of the stairs in the small area between the two wards. He had his back to her, staring through the window. The view was the best one to be had of the hospital gardens and Amanda was glad of his apparent absorption. Perhaps he wouldn't notice as she slipped past. But Jack turned almost as her foot left the top stair. His expression suggested that he, too, was in no mood for the jovial environment. His tone was as cool as his gaze. His question made Amanda pause in astonishment.

'Do you know Graham Baker's wife?' he asked.

'Of course.' Amanda replied, her surprise evident. 'Kay was a nurse here until she had the baby. She's an old friend. It was me who introduced her to Graham.'

'How cosy.' Was it her imagination or did his lip curl to match his disgusted tone? Amanda took a step forward, her arms folding defensively.

'What's that supposed to mean?'

Jack also took a step closer. 'Does she know about you and Graham?'

'Of course she does,' Amanda said dismissively. 'It was over well before she started going out with him.'

'What was?'

'My relationship with Graham. I assume that's what you're referring to.'

'It is.' Jack's eyes narrowed. 'But I wasn't talking about it in the past tense.'

Amanda sighed angrily. 'I have no idea what you're talking about but I can't say I like your tone.' She straightened her arms, her hands curling into fists by her sides. 'What's it got to do with you anyway, Jack?'

'I'd say it has everything to do with me. I saw you out there.' Jack's arm jerked stiffly towards the window. 'Necking,' he added in disgust. 'He's the real reason you dumped me, isn't he?'

'What? You saw… Oh, God.' Amanda snorted with incredulity. 'You saw what you wanted to see, Jack.' She stepped away, shaking her head, but then stopped. She turned and her voice was harsh. 'I don't care what you think about me but don't you dare start any rumours that might upset Kay. This is a small town. Everybody knows somebody and it's all too easy for someone to get hold of the wrong idea and cause trouble by making insinuations.'

'I saw you in the guy's arms!'

'It's called a *hug*,' Amanda snarled. 'It's something people do when they care about each other. Especially when one of them has just lost something that meant a lot to them.' Her voice caught. 'Like a friend.'

Jack's face had emptied of its aggression. 'Is that all I was, Amanda? A *friend*?'

Amanda's dark eyes were dull. There was no hint of the sparkle that had seemed as much a part of her as the cheeky dimples. It indicated an emotional shutdown that chilled Jack more than anything she could say.

'I'm talking about my dog. Ralph.' Amanda's tone was as lifeless as her eyes. 'Graham found he had an advanced and inoperable abdominal malignancy this morning. He didn't let him wake from his anaesthetic.'

'Oh, Mandy. I'm so sorry…' Guilt mingled with Jack's empathy. For an instant he could remember only too vividly the pain of his own loss of Gypsy. His childhood companion had been hit by a car in front of him on the way home from school one day. How could he have been so crass as to suggest she might be having an affair with a married man? So egotistical as to assume that her distress was somehow related to himself?

It was his desperate need for this woman which had sparked the irrational jealousy at the sight of her in someone else's arms. Jack needed an explanation for the pain she had caused by backing away from their relationship. She was the first woman he had ever allowed himself to love—and to trust—so completely. He needed to understand what had happened. He wanted to find some way of drawing her back into his life.

He wanted to close the gap between them. To take her in his arms and let his body undo the damage his words had done. But the opportunity was simply not there. Amanda's withdrawal, her icy self-control, had placed an impenetrable barrier between them. As Amanda turned away again the sounds of the choir moving up the stairs increased. The leader was carrying a tall, lighted candle. Their voices gained strength as they neared the wards.

'''''Tis the season to be jolly...''' The irony was not lost on Jack. He watched Amanda walk away from him. The remembered pain of Gypsy's loss seemed insignificant now.

Dorothy was back in her own room, the high-tech monitoring now deemed unnecessary. The IV line was still in for the administration of her antibiotics, the oxygen mask nearby, but Dorothy's eyes were open and alert and Amanda's arrival was welcomed with her rare smile.

'I hear you sat up with me all night, dear.'

'I fell asleep,' Amanda admitted. 'I did try.'

'Just as well. I still feel very tired myself.'

'You will for a few days yet, but you're well on the road to recovery.'

Dorothy closed her eyes wearily. 'Yes. It's quite a surprise, I must say. Perhaps there's something left I'm supposed to do.'

Amanda spoke quietly. 'Like finding out about your son?'

The old woman's eyes opened swiftly. 'How do you know about that? I've never told anyone.'

'You told me last night. You were feverish. You thought you were back in Ashcroft. It was 1918. You wanted to hold your baby.' Amanda's tone was gentle. She took hold of Dorothy's hand as she spoke.

'Nobody else heard and I'm glad I found out. I can understand only too well what it must mean to you.'

Dorothy's breathing still sounded a little ragged. She nodded slowly. 'Yes. You had the same experience. It's strange, isn't it? The coincidences life presents.'

'Did your baby die too?' Amanda's lip quivered.

'Oh, no. He was very healthy, I think. He could certainly cry loudly enough. I've never forgotten it—the sound of that cry.'

'No. You wouldn't. Do you want to tell me what happened, Dorothy?'

The muted tones of 'Silent Night' filled the small room as Dorothy stared thoughtfully at Amanda.

'Shut the door properly, dear.'

Amanda complied. She helped Dorothy take a sip from her glass of water before she sat beside the bed again.

'I was seventeen,' Dorothy said eventually. 'It was nearly Christmas and there was a ball at Ashcroft. I ended up in a bed. My employer's bed.'

Amanda's jaw dropped. 'He was the father of your baby?'

Dorothy nodded. 'John Armstrong. He was a wonderful man. Very handsome. Very proud of his family and position. But he was bitter as well. His marriage was not happy.'

'Why not?'

'His wife was apparently barren. He desperately wanted an heir. When I finally confessed to my condition he said he would be keeping his child if it was a boy. I was to live in hiding, his wife would fake a pregnancy and after the birth I would be sent back to

Scotland. The only other option was to be turned out onto the streets. He would deny paternity and I would have nowhere to go.'

'Not much of a choice.'

'No choice at all, especially when I was half a world away from my family. John Armstrong was very good at making people do what he wanted. His wife was another matter, though. I heard through the housekeeper—the only other person allowed to know—that Mrs Armstrong flatly refused to raise a bastard.'

Dorothy's voice was weakening. Amanda knew she should leave her to rest but she was driven by curiosity. 'Is he your son, Dorothy—the John Armstrong who's at Ashcroft now?'

'I don't know, dear. That's what I came to find out. He refused to see me and then I got sick. I wanted to know whether his father had ever married again, what his birth date was or whether he had any older brothers.'

'I think I could find that out for you,' Amanda offered. 'I could ask Jack.'

Dorothy sighed. 'I was hoping he might try to find me. That's why I agreed to all the publicity. I thought perhaps that somebody, like the old housekeeper, might have told him the truth. I've looked for him all my life—wherever I've been. He had this mole right beside his left eye. Very distinctive. Do you know, I've looked for it on every man I've ever seen for the first time? I know I'd recognise him, no matter what he looked like or how old he was.'

The carol-singers had another closed door to contend with on the ward. Amanda waited until they'd left before knocking and entering quietly. Charlotte Wallace lay, her face turned away from the door.

'How are you feeling, Charlotte?' The young woman's expression was enough of an answer. Amanda drew a chair close to the bed. 'I can get you something for the pain if you need it.'

This time she received a shake of an uncombed head. A weary and dismissive closing of the eyes. But Amanda didn't go away. She sat silently for a few minutes. This was a very difficult encounter for her and she was unsure how to say what she wanted to say. The tension built until finally Amanda said with a rush, 'I had a baby when I was eighteen. Hannah died less than an hour after she was born.'

Charlotte's eyes opened slowly but she said nothing. 'I wasn't allowed to hold her while she was alive. If somebody had suggested it after she had died I would probably have been as horrified as you were yesterday.' Amanda swallowed painfully. 'I'd never held a dead baby until yesterday. It was the hardest thing I'd ever done.'

Charlotte was crying. 'I'm sorry,' she said brokenly. 'I shouldn't have asked you to stay with me.'

Amanda grasped her hand quickly. 'No, don't be sorry. It was hard and I cried all the way but it was also one of the best things I've ever done.'

'How can you say that?' Charlotte's distress was heart-wrenching.

'It's ten years since I lost my baby,' Amanda said. 'I didn't hold her, didn't name her, didn't bury her. For ten years I've wondered what it would have felt like, what she might have looked like.' Amanda squeezed Charlotte's hand. 'Your little boy is beautiful, Charlotte. He looks perfect.'

'You said you didn't name your baby. But you called her Hannah.'

'Much later,' Amanda said softly. 'My grandmother was an amazing lady. She knew that unless I could make the loss real and come to terms with it I would never get over it. She persuaded me to give her a name. We had a tiny headstone made as a memorial and it sits over an empty plot in the cemetery. I go, every year, to remember. It was Christmas Day that she was born and died. I'll go again tomorrow but it'll be the first time I won't sit and wonder what it would have felt like and what she might have looked like. This time I'll know.' Amanda's words shook as tears interrupted their flow. 'She would have looked just like your son.'

The silence was broken by the two women sobbing. They clung to each other, sharing a grief that nobody else nearby could quite understand. Except, perhaps, Dorothy McFadden. It was Charlotte who pulled away.

'Would you…? Would you bring him to me, Amanda? Not when Brian is here—he couldn't cope with that. Just you and me.'

Amanda made a trip home to her flat later that afternoon. The emptiness hit her as she turned her key in the lock and the pain of losing Ralph was unbearable. Christmas had always been a time for her to remember the saddest parts of her life. This year was going to be so much worse. It would be too easy to allow it to destroy any remaining hope for the future but something in Amanda refused to be pulled under. There had to be a way through all the pain. The reason she had come home seemed like a good first step.

Going to the chest of drawers in her bedroom, Amanda pulled open the bottom drawer and moved her clothes out of the way. She removed a flat, tissue-wrapped item and laid it on her bed, carefully unwrapping the contents—a soft, embroidered cotton nightgown, a tiny hand-knitted white cardigan, booties and a bonnet, all made from the finest merino wool, lovingly knitted by her grandmother in anticipation of the birth of her first grandchild. Never worn, they had never even been unwrapped in the last ten years. Amanda knew she had been keeping them for a reason and now she knew what she was going to do. Charlotte had told her, tearfully, that she couldn't ask Brian to bring any baby clothes into the hospital. He would think it was sick, wanting to dress the baby.

'Is it?' she had queried anxiously. 'I feel guilty even wanting to do it.'

'It's not sick,' Amanda assured her firmly. 'It's very natural—and healthy. And I'll be here with you. We'll do it together.'

And they had. Together they had washed and dressed the tiny baby in the privacy of Charlotte's room, a world away from the festive preparations of the ward on Christmas Eve. They had talked a lot. Charlotte named the baby Benjamin Luke. Amanda had taken some instant photographs and together they had taken an ink print of the tiny hands and feet.

'It doesn't seem much to remember him by,' Amanda commented, 'but it will be precious in the years to come.'

Charlotte asked if she could see Benjamin again the next day and Amanda promised she would make it possible.

'Maybe I can persuade Brian to see him. It would be better if he did, wouldn't it?'

'Only if it's something he's able to cope with.'

'Could you talk to him, Amanda? Try to persuade him?'

'I'll talk to him,' Amanda agreed. 'I'll see how he feels about things first.'

What a way to spend Christmas. Surrounded by death. Amanda carried the tiny, still bundle back through the hospital with Benjamin's face well protected from any curious glances by the folds of the wrap. The only person she encountered, however, was Jack.

'So she did want to see him?' His query was soft.

'Yes.'

'I'm just on my way to check her.'

'I think you'll find she's OK.' Amanda shifted her bundle fractionally. 'A lot better than she was.'

'And are you, Mandy?' Jack's face was sombre. 'Are you OK?'

The caring words, the depth of feeling they conveyed and the searching look of concern folded themselves comfortingly around Amanda. 'I will be,' she whispered. 'Thank you for asking.'

A group of visitors, laden with flowers and gifts, appeared at the end of the corridor. Amanda's arms tightened protectively around her burden and her gaze flicked towards the door that led to the basement. 'I'd better go.'

Still they paused, as though something had been

left unsaid and both were waiting for the other to speak. Amanda licked her suddenly dry lips. Could she do it? Could she ask for some time with Jack? To try and explain. To let him know just how deeply she still felt about him. What if he refused? Amanda hesitated a fraction too long and the visitors came steadily closer.

'Merry Christmas, Doc.'

Jack dragged his eyes away from Amanda to find Donald Fisher beside him. A large beer bottle with tinsel wrapped around its neck was pushed into his hand. 'It's for you,' Donald explained.

'Thanks.' Jack managed a smile. 'I'll save it for when I'm off duty.' He turned back, still smiling, to show Amanda the unexpected gift. The corridor was empty and his smile faded rapidly.

Christmas morning dawned with the soft blue of what promised to be a perfect summer's day. Picking a small basketful of flowers in her tiny garden, Amanda smiled as she thought of all the children that would be excitedly unwrapping roller blades and skateboards. They would have a great day to try them out. The thought made her aware of how lonely she felt without Ralph and she was glad to leave as she set out on her usual Christmas pilgrimage.

The cemetery was deserted. Not many people wished to remind themselves of death on Christmas Day. Amanda was grateful for the familiar solitude. It was a long walk along the beautifully kept grass pathways but Amanda knew exactly where she was going. She passed the row of neatly clipped yew spires and turned left. Recent memorial stones were back to back with the weathered stone blocks of the last century as space in the cemetery had decreased. Amanda looked for the large stone that chronicled the death of a mother and her three children on the same day in 1882. She had often wondered about the disaster which had befallen them. Her grandmother's grave site lay on the other side of the sad mystery.

'Happy Christmas, Gran.' Amanda laid the bunch of flowers she had brought beside the grey marble stone and spent several minutes with the special memories of the love her grandmother, Joan Morrison, had shown her. She'd had her pregnancy to thank for the opportunity to know Joan. Her father had never included his mother in the family and hadn't even shown up for her funeral. Amanda thought of her own mother and her ineffectual attempts to support her daughter which had led to their estrangement. Perhaps it wasn't too late. If Jack had found peace with his father then maybe Amanda could follow his example. She decided to make it a starting point for her New Year's resolutions next week.

Amanda reached out and withdrew a single bloom from the bouquet she had left—a pale pink rosebud— then she turned slowly away. The early morning sunshine had gathered intensity. It was going to be a real scorcher. But Mrs Golder would already be busy in the hospital kitchens. No matter the temperature or the season, or the condition of her feet, the patients of Ashburton General would have their Christmas roast turkey with all the trimmings and the hot plum pudding with custard.

Amanda's feet traced a second familiar route to a corner of the cemetery marked by a large silver birch tree where she stopped at a small, isolated headstone inscribed 'Hannah Morrison, 25 December 1989' and then, simply, 'Never Forgotten.' Amanda tucked the pink rosebud very close to the stone where it was swallowed by a fringe of longer grass. Only she would know it was there. She sat on a nearby bench, lost in the peace of her surroundings and the warmth of the sunshine.

It didn't feel at all morbid to be here. To her surprise Amanda also found that her usual sadness wasn't there either. It must be what she had gone through with Charlotte's baby, Benjamin, she decided. Perhaps, finally, she had been able to let go of her grief. With that knowledge came a new confidence that she, Amanda Morrison, could handle anything that life wanted to throw at her and come out intact. Like Ralph's death. Even the loss of Jack Armstrong's love.

Even the fact that he was now walking towards her along the nearest grass path.

'I followed you,' he explained apologetically as he reached the silver birch. 'I was watching your flat from the hospital, waiting for you to come on duty, and I saw you leave. I hope you don't mind.'

Amanda shook her head. 'Have a seat,' she invited, patting the bench beside her.

Jack paused. Squatting, he reached forward and touched the pink rosebud hidden in the grass. He stared silently at the inscription on the stone for a long minute. Finally he looked up at Amanda.

'Was she your baby?' he asked gently.

'Yes.'

'Did she live only for a day?'

'Only an hour or so. I never got to hold her.'

'Why not?'

'They knew she was going to die. They knew I was an unmarried mother so it didn't really matter anyway. They said it was all for the best.'

Jack rose. It took him only a stride or two to reach the bench and he sat down carefully. 'But it wasn't, was it?'

'No.' Amanda took a long breath, aware of the scent of the recently mown grass. 'I was never allowed to hold my baby—alive or dead. It haunted me.' She gave Jack a direct look. 'That's why I feel so strongly about the whole issue.'

'You must have hated that doctor for what he did.'

'Yes, I did.' Amanda paused, surprised at herself for using the past tense. It was the first time she had ever thought of it in the past. Was it part of this new-found peace? Had the time really come when she could let go and move on? For an instant she wanted to tell Jack everything—why her reaction to his father had been so devastating. But the new feeling was too fragile to subject it to such a test. Not yet. Instead, Amanda sighed softly.

'It's always a difficult time of year for me, Jack. Time to remember the death of a child, the death of a dream, the death of a year. Now I can throw in losing Ralph.' She laughed without amusement. 'God, this time it's even the death of a millennium.'

'No.' Jack gripped her hand hard. 'Not the death. It's the beginning of a new one. A new year. New dreams, too. You've got to have dreams, Amanda. Life has got to keep going. It's like Dorothy McFadden's famous tapestry philosophy. If you don't move on to a new area then you're going to end up with a picture you could fit inside her thimble.'

'Thimble!' Amanda exclaimed. 'Oh, I'd forgotten. I've got to get back. I've got a Christmas present for Dorothy that I wanted to give her before I go on duty.'

'I'd better get going as well. Mrs Bennett isn't very well and I said I'd spend as much time as I could with Dad. I hope she's not coming down with that flu.'

Dorothy was enchanted with her gift. She even managed to eat some of the roast turkey for her dinner. Amanda stayed in the hospital until late in the day, joining in the festivities with an enthusiasm that completely disguised any personal melancholy. She was glad to head for home but amazed to realise that she had, unexpectedly, really enjoyed her day. It was the emptiness of her flat that finally undid her new-found contentment.

The emptiness lasted only a short time, however. By the time she had opened all the windows to air the flat and changed into comfortable shorts and a loose shirt, there came a soft rap at her front door. Jack stood there. He wasn't alone. In his arms he held a puppy—a huge bundle of black fluff, a pair of bright button eyes barely visible above the enormous bow in the yellow silk ribbon around its neck.

'Merry Christmas, Amanda.'

Laughing, Amanda allowed the squirming bundle to be placed in her own arms. The weight was surprising. 'What on earth is it?' she asked.

'A Newfoundland. I got hold of Graham Baker the

day you told me about Ralph.' Jack was watching her face closely. 'I asked him to try and track down a litter of something special. This chap's come from Auckland. He's nearly four months old but it seemed like the right choice.'

Amanda put the puppy down on the floor. He took one end of the ribbon in his mouth and began to run in circles, quickly losing his balance and tumbling over. He looked like a dancing bear. Amanda laughed again.

'That's better.' Jack put a hand to Amanda's cheek and turned her head to face his own. 'I was beginning to wonder if I'd ever see your eyes smile again.'

'There hasn't been much to smile about just lately,' Amanda reminded him.

Jack glanced at the puppy who had abandoned the ribbon in favour of chasing his tail. 'That's what this is all about. New beginnings, instead of death. Instead of clinging to the past.' He cradled Amanda's face with both his hands. 'Can you do that, Mandy? Could you start again?'

She smiled softly. 'I hope so, Jack. I want to.'

Jack's eyes darkened to the deepest shade of blue Amanda had ever seen. 'The only dreams that matter to me now all include you, Amanda Morrison. Do you think *we* could start again too?'

She could feel the pressure of his fingers against her face, could feel the passion in his words. This time her voice deserted her and, having failed to vo-calise her response, Amanda simply nodded. It was enough for Jack. The shadows in his eyes cleared, the muscles in his face and hands relaxed.

'Thank God,' he breathed. As their lips touched

Amanda recognised a new dimension in their communication, a depth that included what had gone before and one that acknowledged there was yet more to come. The spiral into the well-remembered passion was still leashed.

'I can't stay,' Jack apologised. 'Mrs Bennett does have the flu and I've got to get back to look after Dad. I'll have to make some other arrangements for the next few days.'

'Don't worry,' Amanda responded. 'Things should be very quiet and we can call you in for any emergencies. It's the real reason you came back here after all.'

'Is it?' Jack grinned. 'I'd forgotten. I think I came here for something quite different.'

'What's that?'

'To find you.' Jack pulled Amanda back into his arms briefly. 'Will you be all right on your own? Do you want to come back to Ashcroft with me?'

'No,' Amanda said hurriedly, aware of an unpleasant tension at the thought of seeing Jack's father again. Maybe she didn't feel the hatred she had harboured but she wasn't ready to forgive the man. 'Besides, I'm not alone any more, am I?'

They both looked at the enormous black puppy who had just finished making an impressively large puddle in the middle of the carpet.

'Oops. I forgot to tell you, he's not house-trained yet. The breeder was keeping him on in the kennels but I talked her out of it. Do you like him?' he added anxiously. 'It's not too soon, is it?'

'No. It's not too soon. He's exactly what I needed.'

Amanda stood on tiptoe to kiss Jack's cheek. 'Thank you.'

Jack watched the puppy, now leaving a trail of giant wet pawprints on the kitchen floor. 'He hasn't got a name yet either. I thought he might tell you what it is himself.'

Amanda laughed but then her brow furrowed. 'I'm sorry I haven't got a gift for you, Jack.'

'Oh, you've given me one,' Jack told her softly. 'The best gift I could have wished for.' He kissed the tip of her nose and then her forehead. 'You've given me the chance to start again.'

CHAPTER EIGHT

EVEN without concrete evidence Amanda was sure she knew the truth.

John Armstrong, Jack's father, was Dorothy McFadden's son. Amanda was the only person who had the knowledge. The question was, what should she do about it? She told herself she could be wrong. She couldn't remember seeing any mole on the face of the old man and the horror of recognition had etched his features firmly into her memory. Neither had she questioned Jack but he had never mentioned any uncles and she knew the birth dates matched. It was instinct that made her so sure. And if she was right, would it make Dorothy any happier to know that her son was a miserable alcoholic? A man whose marriage had fallen apart, whose son had grown up hating him and whose callous treatment of herself had led to such bitterness that it had confirmed a mistrust of men which had affected the whole direction of her life?

The man was dying. Dorothy herself was still unwell so there was no real chance of them actually meeting. Could she, Amanda, present an impartial view of John Armstrong that focused on something positive? She doubted it. She also doubted that she had the desire to try. Her grief over the loss of her baby might be something she could now put behind her. The hatred she had felt for John Armstrong might have faded but she could never forgive him for the part he had played in that chapter of her life.

Yet, if she didn't forgive him, how could she contemplate a future with his son?

Because her love for Jack was strong enough to overcome the association, she answered herself. Because Jack could not be held responsible for the actions of his father. And because the memories were hers alone and she could deal with them.

'Did you find out for me, dear?' Dorothy queried during one of their lunchtime meetings. 'About Jack's father?'

'I haven't really had the chance to ask yet,' Amanda apologised. 'Jack hasn't been in to work for the last two days. I believe his father may have the flu and is rather seriously ill.'

It was only a partial truth. True, they hadn't seen each other since Christmas Day but Jack had telephoned her on several occasions. Their conversations had centred on the present and, more, on the future. By tacit agreement they'd avoided discussion of the past.

'Will we go to London?' Jack had suggested late in the evening on Boxing Day. 'Is that where you'd like to live?'

'What about the puppy?' Amanda had been in bed. Looking up, she'd seen the large white teeth of the new arrival gleaming as he'd busily enlarged the damage already done to Ralph's old basket.

'It's about time he had a name. Hasn't he told you what it is yet?'

Amanda had laughed. 'Nothing very complimentary suggests itself. He's a monster. I've never seen such a force of destruction. He charges around here like a bull in a china shop. I might call him Holocaust.'

'Call him Jefferson.'

'Why?'

'Donald Fisher has a prize bull called Jefferson.'

'I'm kind of hoping he'll grow out of his bull-like attributes. But I quite like the name.'

'Let's just hope he doesn't develop Jefferson's more notable attributes.'

'Like what?'

'Think about it. You've lived in the country long enough.'

Amanda giggled. 'Is this degenerating into an obscene phone call?'

'What a good idea. Seeing as I'm stuck here, I may as well tell you—in intimate detail—exactly what I'm planning the next time I get you alone. In bed, preferably.'

Amanda snuggled further under the bed covers, the phone clutched firmly against her ear. 'I'm in bed already,' she whispered.

'Are you wearing anything?'

'Only the phone,' Amanda said huskily.

The sharp intake of breath on the other end of the line suggested that the information had had considerable effect. It was some time later that Amanda reluctantly replaced the receiver. Smiling blissfully, she stared at the ceiling. What did it matter that they hadn't got back to discussing where they might live? As long as they were together the location was an insignificant detail for her.

Apparently it wasn't so insignificant to Jack. Their

conversation the following evening had returned to the subject.

'You wouldn't marry me just for my money, would you, Mandy?'

'I don't know. Have you got any?'

'Quite a bit. I never bothered buying any property. I put my savings into the share market and they've done rather well. Not well enough for what I'm thinking of doing with it but it would be a good start.'

'What are you planning to buy?'

'Ashcroft.'

Amanda had gasped. It wasn't something she had even remotely considered the possibility of. 'But you hate being here! Small town, small minds, remember? You'd be bored stiff.'

'I wanted to feel like that. The reality has proved a bit different. Kevin Farrow tells me there are no takers for the permanent surgical post yet. He's having trouble even finding another locum.'

'But…' Amanda was struggling, wondering how she would cope with the very idea of living in John Armstrong's house. 'But you hate the house. You said it was destined to be destroyed—along with the Armstrong family.'

'And you said you loved it. That there must be some way to save it. That it was worth preserving at any cost.'

'Yes…I did.' But she'd had no idea that the cost might be a personal one.

'Think of all the room Jefferson would have to run around in. Think of how many kids we could have to fill up the bedrooms. We could bring it to life again,

Mandy. Fill it with happy memories. Think of the name in the window. I think we belong there.'

And Amanda *had* remembered the window. Remembered the overwhelming feeling that Jack had belonged in that house. 'It wouldn't be easy,' she said tentatively, not quite sure exactly what she was referring to. Probably her own reaction to the idea, but Jack agreed readily.

'Even if I could afford the house I probably couldn't manage any repairs. I don't even know who actually owns the property. The paperwork only lists a conglomerate called Starbright International. Some sort of tourist enterprise, the farm manager tells me. I guess I've had too much time to think about it. I haven't even set foot outside for two days.'

Amanda was grateful for the conversational escape route. 'How is your father? Is it flu, do you think?'

It was the flu. On top of the advancing malignancy and complications it was enough for John Armstrong to need admission to hospital with bronchial pneumonia by the afternoon of the twenty-eighth. It was quite obvious that a discharge was a remote possibility. John Armstrong's time had come and the task of the medical staff was simply to make him as comfortable as possible. Amanda was still on duty but avoided involvement with the admission. Now Dorothy McFadden and her son were separated by only a matter of a short corridor. Amanda could think of little else. She buried herself in paperwork but couldn't concentrate.

Escaping home when her shift ended, Amanda found plenty of distraction in feeding and playing with Jefferson and cleaning up the debris from his day's activities. She filled in the holes he had dug in the lawn, sighed over the remnants of the automatic watering system and ruefully eyed the ragged remains of the washing she had imprudently hung on the line. Then she found the culprit inside, shredding the rolled-up newspaper she had prepared as a means of discipline.

'You do need more space,' she told the pup. 'This is no place for you.'

It wasn't the place for her just then either. Amanda was drawn back to the hospital. She hadn't seen Jack yet and she knew that, however much she hated the idea, she needed to see John Armstrong once more. She had to know whether it would be possible to forgive him and she couldn't know that unless she saw him face to face.

Jack was sitting in an armchair. He looked exhausted and Amanda's heart squeezed painfully at his distressed expression. No matter how much it was expected, it was very hard to lose a parent. With the complicated emotional relationship Jack had with his father, it was only going to be more difficult. Amanda was surprised to find John Armstrong awake and lucid. Perhaps his condition was not yet as critical as reports had suggested.

Jack stood up as Amanda closed the door behind her. She went to him and took his outstretched hand in her own. Jack pulled her close and hugged her hard. 'I'm glad you came,' he told her softly.

The muffled sounds from the bed made Jack release his hold on Amanda. He lifted the oxygen mask from his father's face. 'What did you say, Dad?'

'Who's that?'

'It's Amanda Morrison.'

Amanda stepped forward. 'Hullo, Dr Armstrong. How are you feeling?'

'I'm dying, that's how I'm feeling. Go away.'

Amanda caught Jack's eye and stepped back, relieved at the dismissal.

'Wait.' It was the old man who spoke. 'You're Joan Morrison's granddaughter, aren't you?'

'Yes, I am.'

'I thought I'd seen you before.' John was panting, his words coming between painful rasps of breath. 'You had a baby.'

Amanda's heart jerked painfully. There was no way to avoid it now. 'Yes,' she admitted softly.

John seemed to be having a difficult struggle with his breathing. Jack reached for the oxygen mask but his father pushed his hands away. 'Why is she here, Jack? I don't need to be reminded of how I failed.'

Jack's sharp look at Amanda made her afraid. Afraid of his anger when he discovered what she had been hiding.

'I'd better go,' she whispered. John's eyes had closed. Perhaps he was beyond telling Jack anything else and she could then explain at a more appropriate time. But his eyes flickered open again as she moved.

'I failed her child. I failed my own child.' Amanda stared in horror as she saw the slow tears ooze from the dying man's eyes. 'I'm sorry, Jack.'

'I know.' Jack had caught hold of his father's hand.

'There was nothing more I could have done.'

Oh, yes, there was, Amanda thought angrily. There was a lot more but you chose not to do it. She stared at the drawn face on the pillow, willing his eyes to

open again and for him to say something to her.
Something that might ignite a spark of forgiveness on
her part. But his eyes remained shut. She saw the
faded scar beside his left eye as she stared. A small
scar, almost invisible. You'd have to be looking for
it to notice. The sort of scar that would be left after
the removal of a mole. Amanda was aware of his
breath sounds becoming quieter. The blip of the cardiac monitor jumped erratically and then slowed a
little.

'Why didn't you tell me?' Jack whispered. 'Did
you think I wouldn't understand how you felt about
him?'

'You were sorting out your own problems with
him,' Amanda said reluctantly. 'I didn't want to spoil
the understanding you were coming to. He *was* your
father, Jack.'

Jack was silent for a minute, before speaking
gently. 'He trained in a time when it would have been
unthinkable to let a mother hold a dead or dying baby,
Amanda. He probably thought he was helping you.'

Amanda was silent. She transferred her gaze back
to the figure on the bed. To reach the end of a life
and to be filled with a sense of failure was dreadful.
She pitied John Armstrong. With the sense of pity
came a resolution that she would not allow life to
control her the same way. She would not allow the
past to control any part of her future. When her time
eventually came she wanted to be proud of what she
had achieved. And she wanted to have the love of a
family surrounding her.

Amanda stepped forward again and slid her hand
into Jack's, her eyes filling with tears. She could feel

the loneliness of John's departure despite having his son beside him. He had missed out on the most important thing life had to offer and she felt desperately sorry for him. With the sorrow came, at last, a genuine regret that she had laid so much blame at his feet. She could—*did*—forgive him.

It was almost as though he had waited for her to find that resolution. The alarm on the monitor signalled the absence of an indrawn breath and the cardiac monitor followed suit as the arrhythmia flickered and then settled into a straight line. Jack turned the alarms off.

'He requested no attempt at resuscitation.' There was an absolute silence and then Jack sighed heavily as he placed his father's hand gently on the bed. 'I guess he's at peace now.'

'Yes,' Amanda agreed with a catch in her voice. And he wasn't the only one.

Jack touched the tears on her cheeks with a wondering expression and Amanda saw the glint of moisture in his own eyes as he understood their meaning. They stood together, holding each other tightly, acknowledging the influence John Armstrong had had on both their lives, the hatred he had generated and the forgiveness they could both now share.

It was still light at 9 p.m. With formal duties and arrangements over with, Jack and Amanda found themselves walking in the hospital gardens as he took her home. Dusk had softened the light and strengthened the scent from the rose beds. The sporadic, final evening calls of the birds was the only sound until Amanda spoke.

'I have a confession to make, Jack. It concerns your father and I feel rather guilty about it.'

'Me, too. I feel more than a little guilty.'

'Do you?' Amanda was surprised. Perhaps Jack already knew what she had to tell him. 'You first,' she prompted.

'OK.' Jack sat down on a bench and pulled Amanda down beside him. 'When Dad died I wasn't even thinking about him. I had been thinking how pointless his life had been and what a miserable ending to it and then all I could think about was you.' Jack caught Amanda's hand and pressed it to his lips. 'I felt an overwhelming love for you and knew that I would die as miserably as my father unless I had you beside me and knew that you had loved me as much as I love you.' Jack grinned suddenly, lightening his tone. 'I'd prefer some representatives of another couple of generations around as well, mind you.'

Amanda rested her head on Jack's shoulder. 'That's amazing. I felt the same thing. And I felt horribly sorry for your father not having that. It was then that I found I could really forgive him. It doesn't matter what he did. It's up to me how I let it affect my life.'

'Exactly. He's been my excuse to avoid relationships and never put down roots. I've wasted a lot of years.'

'Just as well.' Amanda smiled. 'Or I'd never have met you. You couldn't have put down roots anyway where you were. They're already here—at Ashcroft. Which brings me to my confession.'

'I thought that was it. Hadn't we better go and see if your house is still intact? Jefferson's been on his own for a while.'

'In a minute. Did you know that John Armstrong was the father of Dorothy McFadden's baby?'

Jack snorted with disbelief. 'He was a bit young for her, wasn't he? When was this?'

'Nineteen-eighteen. I'm talking about your grandfather, not your father. It's confusing, you all having the same name.'

'Family tradition. We'll have to call our first son John as well.'

'Perhaps it's time to start some new traditions.'

'Such as?'

'Having daughters.'

'Great idea. We'll call her Joan—after your grandmother. That way we won't have to change the initials on the family silverware.' Jack put his lips close to Amanda's ear. 'Let's go and do something about it. Now.' His lips sought Amanda's as she turned her head but the kiss was tender, a gentle pressure that spoke of caring and commitment more than passion. Amanda pulled away.

'It wouldn't feel right just now, Jack. Your father's—'

But Jack shook his head, cutting off her words. 'I can't think of a better time to start a new life,' he said. 'Figuratively and literally. You and me...' His eyebrow lifted suggestively. 'And little Joan.'

Amanda sighed, tempted, but when Jack moved to pull her close again she gave him a small push. 'Listen, Jack. I'm trying to tell you something important here.'

'I'm listening. Make it quick, eh?'

'Right. Dorothy McFadden is your grandmother.'

'What?'

'Listen…' Amanda began to tell him Dorothy's incredible story. He soon began nodding and his expression was grim when he broke in.

'It all fits. He knew.'

'He did? Then I *should* have told him. He could have met his mother.'

'No.' Jack shook his head quickly. 'I don't mean he knew the truth. He knew his mother had never wanted him—hated him even. And his father had seen him simply as the heir. He wanted more than that. That's why he insisted on doing medicine and not just taking over the farm. But he got sucked back. The property had always been more important than him. He told me all this that night you walked out on me and we sat up all night, talking. Now I understand how it happened. He was right. His mother did hate him.'

'He wasn't even her child.' Amanda nodded. 'He must have had a miserable upbringing.'

'He never learned how to love anything except Ashcroft. Goodness knows why my mother fell for him but I think she came to understand that she wasn't as important as the property. It was the ultimate revenge—removing the heir.'

'And he lost the property as well. No wonder he didn't care any more about what happened. And no wonder alcohol got such a grip on him.'

'He never expected me to show up again,' Jack said heavily. 'Never wanted me to. He didn't want to have to face up to his failures.'

'Dorothy's last wish was to meet her son. It's why she came back. I could have brought them together and I didn't because of how I felt about him. Now the opportunity has gone.'

'It was never there,' Jack informed her. 'It would never have worked. My father has never known real love. He would have blamed Dorothy for allowing him to be given such a miserable childhood. I'm sure she feels badly enough about it without the guilt that extra knowledge would contribute.'

'But she never even saw her son!'

'No. But she could meet her grandson. Do you think she might be happy with that?'

Dorothy McFadden was more than happy with that.

Amanda was so proud of the way Jack had introduced himself to the old woman. Recovered enough from her pneumonia to be sitting out on the verandah and enjoying some sunshine, Amanda had made sure they would be undisturbed when Jack paid his first visit on the afternoon of the twenty-ninth. She hadn't given Dorothy any advance warning and was now a little worried about the potential effects of the surprise. Her hesitation resulted in an awkward silence when she closed the doors, after ushering Jack onto Ward 2's verandah.

It was Jack who took over the introduction. 'I'm Jack Armstrong,' he told Dorothy gently, taking hold of the shaking hand that still clasped the tapestry needle. 'I believe I have the pleasure of meeting my grandmother?'

It was Jack who held Dorothy while she came to grips with the emotional overload. It was Jack who fished through the needlework bag and found the fresh handkerchief to mop up her tears. And it was

Jack who talked, quietly and reassuringly, until Dorothy's questions began to flow.

Jack produced a large manila envelope which Amanda saw was stuffed with old sepia photographs and faded-looking papers. 'I was very late for work this morning,' he said with a smile. 'It was rather fascinating, sorting through some of the boxes in the study. This is only a small sample but I think most of it dates to the time you were at Ashcroft, Dorothy. I suspect it's more than enough to be going on with.'

'That's your grandfather!' Dorothy said, excitedly reaching for one the photographs as Jack tipped the contents onto the table. 'That's exactly how I remember him. Oh, he was a handsome man!'

Amanda slipped quietly away. She would love to share the memories and learn more about both Ashcroft and the earlier generations of Armstrongs, but she would have plenty of time for that. Amanda was smiling as she closed the verandah doors quietly behind her. This was something special between Jack and his grandmother. A time just for them to find a bond. Dorothy McFadden had only a limited time left to share with her grandson.

Amanda could look forward to sharing the rest of her life with him.

CHAPTER NINE

It wasn't just the pin-striped suit and tie that was making Kevin Farrow look so uncomfortable. It was more the difficulty he was having trying to convey his message through the interpreter for the busload of Japanese tourists.

'No visitors,' he enunciated deliberately. 'Miss McFadden is sleeping.' He put his hands together and laid his cheek on them. The babble of the alien language from the small crowd increased. Kevin, now backed up against the main staircase, cast a despairing glance over the heads of the would-be sightseers. Seeing Amanda's and Karen's amused expressions as they both watched from behind the safety of the reception desk, he mouthed what looked like an appeal for assistance. Amanda held her hands up, palms outwards, suggesting that there was nothing she could do. She grinned at Karen.

'Time I escaped upstairs and went on duty, I think.'

A platinum blonde head moved past the sea of black hair as a newcomer glided towards the desk. 'I just adore your hospital. It's so *cute*!'

Amanda's smile broadened. The American accent was perfect. The woman could win a Barbie lookalike competition. She was accompanied by a team, carrying cameras and sound equipment. 'We'll just set up over there, by all the cards and flowers,' Amanda was informed. 'I just *love* that pile of gifts.'

Amanda nodded. It was all totally beyond her control. Kevin might have been excitedly anticipating all the expected attention the hospital was to receive, but the reality was leaving them all stunned. It was nearly 4 p.m. on New Year's Eve and the whiteboard was counting off the hours instead of days. A courier van could be seen edging past the bus that was blocking most of the driveway outside the main entrance. A new load of flowers and gifts began to be unloaded.

Karen nudged Amanda. 'What on earth are we going to do with it all?'

'Dorothy wants everything distributed to local charities and residential homes. Kevin's arranged for a delivery firm to come after New Year's Day.'

Another film crew moved past the desk. The language sounded European. Amanda shook her head. 'We've got to do something about this crowd. What would happen if we got some sort of emergency?'

The shriek from a Japanese woman that punctuated Amanda's sentence was alarming to say the least. It was immediately followed by more cries of dismay and the group of tourists moved back from the stairs as one body. Kevin had a look on his face that bordered on panic. Surely he couldn't have said anything that culturally insensitive? Amanda's gaze travelled swiftly past the administrator to the mercifully unpopulated stairs.

'Oh, *no*!' Amanda's groan was wrenched out of her. Then she stared in disbelief. Heads all over the foyer had begun to turn at the sound of the tourists' alarm. Now pockets of conversation died and only the American frontwoman continued, standing before the display of birthday cards, oblivious to everything except the camera. Then she, too, stopped abruptly.

'What the…?'

The stairs had been empty. Kevin had been staunchly protecting access to the wards but he hadn't allowed for an approach from above. And he certainly hadn't allowed for it in the form of Jim Cooper. Jim had outdone himself this time. He had his hat on, of course, and also a pair of heavy farm workboots. In his hand he brandished the new electric razor his family had given him for Christmas. These accessories were his only attire. Between the hat and the boots Jim Cooper was stark naked. It had taken only seconds from the first tourist shriek to an absolute, stunned silence.

'Bloody shearing gangs,' Jim shouted angrily into the silence. 'You're all useless! Can't you see it's going to rain?'

Another figure leaped down the stairs. Jack was removing his white coat as he moved. He managed to wrap it around Jim Cooper in the instant before the American crew finished repositioning their cameras. Amanda gave him a thumbs-up sign as he turned the old man and began guiding him back up the stairs with an arm firmly around his shoulders.

The tour guide and interpreter both began talking loudly. The tourists obediently turned and hurried back to the main entrance, several woman fanning their faces with their hands. The Barbie doll was talking excitedly to her cameraman but he was shaking his head sadly over the apparently missed footage. Amanda was laughing as she moved through the rapidly clearing space towards Kevin.

'You look like you could use a stiff drink.'

Kevin checked his watch. 'Only two hours and that's exactly what I'll be doing.'

'Are the security arrangements all sorted for to-night?'

Kevin nodded. 'The action will all be at the street party so I don't think we'll have problems. The entertainment starts at 8 p.m. We'll lock up tight after visiting hours and nobody's allowed near Dorothy. She needs all the rest she can get before the press conference tomorrow.'

'Where are you holding it?'

'Here—in the foyer. It's the largest space we've got. We're going to put a temporary platform at the bottom of the stairs here with an armchair for Dorothy. The builders are coming in at 6 a.m. to get set up.' He looked hopefully at Amanda. 'Any news?'

Amanda tried to look stern. 'What about, Kevin?'

Kevin grinned. 'You know perfectly well.'

'And you know nothing's going to change. We have no one anywhere near due for delivery that we know about. You're not going to get the first baby for the year delivered here, Kevin. Give it up.'

Kevin sighed sadly. 'People all over the world have been timing conception and even arranging Caesareans to get in on the right day. Why couldn't someone around here have been a bit more co-operative? I did try to talk Linda into it back in March,' he added wistfully. 'But she wasn't having a bar of it.'

Amanda had to laugh. 'I'm not surprised. Haven't you got enough on your plate as it is?'

'I guess. Hey!' Kevin punched Amanda's arm

lightly. 'What's this I hear about you and Jack Armstrong? Are you really getting married tomorrow?'

'Mmm.' Amanda rolled her eyes. 'I didn't think it was such a good idea but Jack was inspired and found a Justice of the Peace who could get through the red tape and make arrangements. It's only going to be a quiet affair in the hospital chapel. Your invitation's in your letter-box. I delivered them this afternoon before I came on duty.' The invitations had all been local and easily delivered by hand—all except one, which Amanda had posted yesterday. She could only hope that her mother would receive it in time and see beyond the occasion to the invitation to make a new start in their relationship.

'What time is the big event?'

'Six p.m.'

Kevin's eyes brightened. 'Couldn't you make it a bit earlier? Say, lunchtime—while all the television crews are still here?'

'No way. This is private,' Amanda warned. 'And don't you dare try to make it anything else, Kevin.' Then she relaxed her sharp tone and smiled triumphantly. 'Otherwise I might just issue an invitation for Jim Cooper to attend the press conference.'

Kevin's forecast had been accurate. Even visiting hours were much quieter than usual, with the festivities getting under way in and around the town domain. The hospital seemed strangely cut off after the locking of the main doors but Amanda enjoyed the peaceful night-time drug round at 9 p.m.

'You could go to the street party, you know, Jack.

You don't have to hang around here to keep me company.' Amanda dropped the pills she had just collected into a tiny paper cup which she handed to the ward nurse. 'That's for Mrs Orchard, Colleen. Make sure she takes them with plenty of water and she can have a sleeping pill if she really thinks she's going to need it.'

Jack pulled his elbows behind his back as he stretched. 'I'm just going to go and say goodnight to Dorothy. Want to come with me?'

'Sure.' Amanda recorded the drugs dispensed on the chart and waved at Colleen. 'I'll be in with Dorothy if you need me,' she called.

Supper had been served during the drug round and Dorothy hurriedly put down her mug of hot chocolate. 'Jack! How lovely of you to come and see me again. And Amanda. Why aren't you both at the big party?'

Amanda used a tissue to mop up the puddle of spilt chocolate on Dorothy's locker. 'We'd rather visit you,' she stated.

'We're saving our strength for tomorrow,' Jack added. He and Dorothy exchanged a smile.

They had spent a lot of time together over the last few days and Amanda had been thrilled at the easy rapport they had established.

'We won't stay long.' Amanda pulled up a chair and sat down. Jack rested an arm along its back. 'You need to rest as well.'

'I'm feeling so much better,' Dorothy declared. 'And Doctor Garrett says I can start weight-bearing on my heel now. He's talking about discharging me.'

'That's wonderful!'

Jack was frowning. 'Where would you go?'

'I won't go far,' Dorothy said thoughtfully. 'I've only just discovered a grandson. I'd like a little more time to get to know him.'

'I've got something for you,' Amanda said shyly. She fished in her pocket and drew out a wedding invitation. 'It's a bit short notice, I'm afraid.'

Dorothy opened the envelope and read the card it contained.

Amanda's tone was anxious. 'You may be too tired after all the people coming in the morning but I— *we*—would really love you to be there.'

'You're the only family I have now,' Jack said persuasively.

'And just think,' Amanda added excitedly. 'When Jack and I are married you'll be my real grandmother.'

'I wouldn't miss this for anything in the world.' Dorothy folded the card and clasped it close to her chest. 'I've been telling Amanda she needed more colour in her life. I'm so happy for you both.'

'Our first daughter is going to be called Joan.' Jack grinned. 'After Amanda's grandmother. Maybe we'll call the next one Dorothy. What do you think, Mandy?'

'Won't fit the silverware,' Amanda pointed out. She and Jack exchanged a laughing glance and Dorothy, watching them both carefully, nodded to herself with satisfaction. Then the lines around her mouth deepened as she frowned.

'I won't have time to find a wedding gift for you.'

Jack and Amanda transferred their gaze. 'You're not to spend any money on us,' Jack told her firmly.

'You keep it for yourself.' His brow creased with concern. 'Are you all right? I mean financially?'

'Oh, yes, dear. Despite my stepchildren's best efforts they weren't able to take everything from me. In particular, I have a property holding that my first husband bought in my name. The income from that has been more than enough to keep me very comfortably off.'

'First husband?' Amanda was open-mouthed. 'How many have you had?'

'Only two. I married Douglas in 1920. We were very happy for more than thirty years.'

'But you had no children?' Amanda was fascinated. Despite all the interviews Dorothy McFadden had managed to keep large sections of her life quite private.

'No, dear. I suspect something went wrong after the birth of my son.' She glanced at Jack. 'Of your father. I got very sick on the ship going home. They said I almost died.'

'Tell me about Douglas,' Amanda urged. 'What did he do?'

'Oh, all sorts of things. Property development mainly. He liked to find what he called ''spots of potential'' and build them up into tourist resorts. People would tell him about places and we'd travel to see them. It was an exciting life. We came to New Zealand around 1950 and he purchased an area in the Bay of Islands. Beautiful place.' Dorothy fell silent as though lost in her recollections.

'And your second husband?' prompted Jack. He was leaning on the back of Amanda's chair, as fascinated as she was.

'Oh, that wasn't so wonderful. I suspect he married me for my money. That was certainly all his children were interested in after he died. But that's twenty years ago now. I've been quite happy on my own. I still travelled a lot. I love cruise ships. You feel very free to go anywhere when you have no family to consider and enough money not to be a burden on anyone.'

'You have family now,' Amanda said quietly. 'And you'll never be a burden.'

'That's right,' Jack agreed. 'We want to look after you now, Dorothy. No more travelling.'

Amanda twisted her face upwards and caught Jack's eye. He nodded and his tone was serious as he turned back to his grandmother. 'Amanda and I have discussed this,' he told Dorothy. 'We'd like you to come and live with us.'

Dorothy blinked in surprise. 'Oh, I don't think that would be possible.'

'Why not?' The two voices spoke in unison.

'Your flat is much too small for that. No, I'll go back to the hotel.'

'We're not going to live in my flat,' Amanda laughed. 'Jack has plans.'

Jack nodded and took a long, indrawn breath. 'It's probably too soon to say anything because I don't know how successful I'll be but...' He paused and nodded, as though confirming his own ambition. 'I'm...*we're* going to try and buy Ashcroft. The house, anyway.'

'It's where the Armstrongs belong,' Amanda finished softly. 'And we're going to make it a happy place again.'

*   *   *

'What made her cry, do you think?' Jack leaned back in the ward office chair, his feet propped up on the desk.

'I'm not sure,' Amanda replied. 'Maybe it's the thought of being part of a family—of having a grandson who cares about her.'

'I wonder if she'll live long enough to see her first great-grandchild?'

'I hope so. Wouldn't it be perfect if he was born at Ashcroft?'

'No way. I'm not having anything to do with a home birth, thank you. And it's a she, not a he. A boy will never cope with being called Joan.'

'He could be Joe,' Amanda reasoned smilingly. 'Do you think it's possible?'

'I'd say there's about a fifty per cent chance.' Jack was grinning broadly.

Amanda gave him a mildly exasperated look. 'I don't mean the sex. I mean being at Ashcroft when we have our first baby.'

Jack looked more serious. 'I'm making progress. My solicitor has tracked down the agents for Starbright International. They're a British legal firm. We're just waiting to hear back to find the name of the actual owner.'

'They can't be very interested if they've never even been here,' Amanda suggested hopefully. 'Maybe they'll sell cheaply.'

'Let's hope so or we might have to live with sub-standard plumbing till we're as old as Dorothy.'

'Well, we could—' Amanda's speculation was interrupted by the telephone ringing beside her. She glanced at her watch as she replaced the receiver a short time later. 'We could be in for a busy couple of hours after all.'

'Why? The wards are almost empty.'

'There's a crowd of about thirty thousand at the domain. The casualties started arriving about half an hour ago and Chris is yelling for help. He's got a man with chest pain who just came in and could be infarcting and an asthma case on the way. He can't raise Colin on his cellphone. If he's at the domain he probably can't even hear it.'

'I'll come down with you.'

'That would be great. There's a child with severe abdominal pain as well.'

The child turned out to be young Jason Cotter. The aversion he had developed towards medical procedures, thanks to his tonsillectomy, would make examination difficult and having a considerable wait in which to contemplate the awful possibilities led to a gradual increase in the noise level emanating from his cubicle.

Jack took over the management of the teenager with asthma that Robert Bayliss brought in as they arrived.

'She's dosed herself with her Ventolin inhaler a couple of times.'

'How long ago?'

Robert checked his watch. 'First one would have been twenty minutes ago. Another dose ten minutes ago. I thought I'd better bring her straight in rather than muck about getting an IV line in. I've had her on oxygen. No salbutamol yet.'

'Thanks, Bob.' They transferred the terrified girl

onto the bed and Jack smiled reassuringly. 'What's your name, love?'

She was barely able to get the sound of a word out through her struggle to breathe but Jack just caught it. 'OK, Jane. We'll get you sorted out, don't worry.' He nodded at the nurse. 'Have you set up the salbutamol nebuliser?' He took the mask she was holding. 'And draw up some aminophylline, thanks—250 mg in 10 ml.'

Amanda blocked out the sounds of Jason's anxiety as she helped Chris with the middle-aged man suffering chest pain. The twelve-lead ECG was reassuring. It seemed to be a severe angina attack rather than an infarct. With blood-thinning agents and beta-blockers to address the cause of his symptoms and narcotic pain relief, nitrates and oxygen to deal with the effects, his condition improved considerably but he would still need close observation for a while.

Robert's ambulance was back fifteen minutes later. A three-year-old girl had fallen from a merry-go-round and had a suspected broken collar-bone. Amanda made several phone calls, managing to get hold of two extra nursing staff, the radiologist on call and finally making contact with Colin Garrett. The background noise level of the domain festivities made conversation difficult but Colin got the message he was needed.

Amanda then went in to see Jason. The three-year-old girl's screams had masked the fact that Jason had miraculously quietened down but the explanation made itself obvious even before Amanda entered the cubicle. The small boy had been copiously sick.

'What on earth have you been eating, Jason?'

'What hasn't he been eating?' his mother groaned.
'Hot dogs, chips, Coke, ice cream. You name it—he's
eaten it.'

'How many hot dogs did you have, Jason?'

'Six,' he announced proudly. 'Dad bought me some
more when Mum wasn't looking.'

'Well, no wonder you had such a sore tummy.'

'I feel better,' Jason stated. 'Can we go now, Mum?
I don't want to miss the fireworks.'

Amanda looked up at the clock. Eleven-thirty. The
fireworks were still half an hour away. 'Let's keep
him here just for another fifteen minutes,' she suggested to Jason's mother. 'If he still feels fine then
you can go and you'll still be in time for the
fireworks.'

A badly sprained ankle came in as Jason was leaving. 'I was dancing,' the owner explained. 'And I fell
off the box.'

Jack pushed the lock of hair back from his forehead
as he grinned. 'Why were you dancing on top of a
box?'

'It was the only way to see the band. Can I just get
it bandaged or something so I can get back for the
fireworks?'

'We'll need to take an X-ray,' Jack told her. 'It's
a nasty-looking sprain and it could well be fractured.'
Then he smiled understandingly at her disappointed
expression. 'Tell you what. If we put you in a wheel-
chair I'm sure someone will be more than happy to
take you up to one of the verandahs. You'll get a good
view from up there.' The nurse assisting him nodded
eagerly. No one wanted to miss the display.

Jack went hunting for Amanda. 'My asthmatic is

well under control,' he told her. 'Colin's going to admit her for observation overnight. Would you like to go upstairs and see the fireworks?' The muted, but loud explosions could already be heard inside the emergency department.

Amanda shook her head apologetically. 'Robert just called. He's bringing in a woman in labour.'

'You're kidding! Is it premature? I thought we didn't have any due for weeks.'

'We don't. She's down from Christchurch for the party. Thirty-eight weeks gestation so she didn't think it was too much of a risk. Apparently she was having such a good time she ignored the signs until her waters broke.'

Jack shook his head. 'Kevin must have friends on high,' he commented drily.

'You go upstairs,' Amanda urged. 'If you run you'll see the last of it. It'll be the most excitement you'll get in Ashburton for quite some time.'

Jack's eyes hooded slightly. He leaned forward and breathed heavily in Amanda's ear. 'Don't you believe it, woman. We've got a week's honeymoon coming up, remember?'

'Mmm.' Amanda gave a very feminine smile. 'There is that.' She looked up as the doors to the ambulance bay opened. 'Still, you don't need to stay for this. I'll call you if we run into any problems.'

'I'll stay,' Jack said decisively. 'I need the practice.' He cast Amanda a stern glance. 'Just in case you do decide to produce Joan in the ancestral hall.'

The baby wasn't going to make headlines by being the first arrival for the millennium. It was nearly 2 a.m. when the new arrival put in her appearance.

For a minute it looked as though they might be in trouble. The baby was blue and limp. Amanda moved in quickly with the suction equipment.

'It's a girl,' she called to the excited mother, who struggled to sit herself up further.

'Let me see her!' she cried. 'I want to hold her.'

There was a moment's silence as Jack caught Amanda's eye. Jack was still holding the baby he had insisted on delivering himself. As Amanda pulled the suction tube away the baby moved, opened its mouth and gave a gurgling, choked cry.

The mother's voice rose in panic. 'What's the matter with her? Why can't I hold her?'

Jack straightened, still holding the baby, the cord unclamped. As the baby drew in a new breath a pink tinge rapidly began to replace the blue. Jack placed the baby gently on the mother's draped abdomen and caught her outstretched hand, guiding it down to touch her infant.

'Of course you can hold her,' he said gently. His eyes met Amanda's again. 'I wouldn't dream of stopping you.'

CHAPTER TEN

'HEY, Amanda!'

Amanda was pulled to a halt by the firm tug on her hand. She and Jack were negotiating a now-familiar route through the darkened hospital grounds. Her heart suddenly beat faster at Jack's tone. Had he spotted something? Surely Jim Cooper hadn't managed to engineer another escape from the ward and was now lurking in the rose beds?

'What is it?' she queried breathlessly.

Jack let go of her hand and tapped his watch. 'It's the year two thousand,' he told her gravely.

'So it is! In fact, it must be about three hours old by now.'

'And Armageddon hasn't arrived.'

'Don't be too sure.' Amanda's lips curved into a wide smile. 'We're not home yet and Jefferson has had the place to himself.'

'I love you,' Jack said, his tone still solemn.

'I love you, too. Happy New Year, Jack.'

'Mmm. I believe there's a more traditional way of communicating that wish.'

'Yes!' Amanda's face lit up. 'I've got it all ready. Come on!' She grabbed Jack's hand and tugged him into a run despite his protests that he had something else in mind.

Jefferson was soundly asleep, safely incarcerated in Amanda's laundry. Having peeped through the window to check on him, Amanda bypassed the house and made for the garden shed. Intrigued, Jack followed her, watching as she retrieved a flat package and a box of matches.

'I knew I'd miss the fireworks,' she explained, 'so I got these from Mr Harris at the hardware store last week. He had some left over from Guy Fawke's Day.'

'Skyrockets?' Jack eyed the very flat package dubiously.

'Sparklers!' Amanda said triumphantly. 'Here…' She put two wire sticks into Jack's hand and scraped a match alight. The tips of the sparklers glowed, sputtered and then burst into fountains of white stars. She took one and held it aloft.

'Happy New Year, Jack!'

'Does this mean I don't get my kiss?' Jack's expression was one of joyous delight as he watched the brilliance of the fireworks reflected in Amanda's dark eyes.

In response, Amanda held her sparkler further away and tilted her head up towards Jack. The hiss and pop of the sparklers was the only sound as their lips met and the glowing wires had long since died to a blackened curl by the time they separated. Jack's lips still hovered close, brushing Amanda's ear and then nuzzling her neck.

'You should go home,' she told him huskily.

'You wouldn't be so cruel!' The lips nudged her collar aside and explored the dip of her collar-bone.

'We're getting married tomorrow!' Amanda protested.

'Exactly.'

'You're not supposed to see the bride the night before the wedding. It's bad luck.'

'Sure is,' Jack murmured. His hand glided up to softly brush and settle on Amanda's breast as his lips moved to her throat. She gave a sigh of pleasure which quickly became a frustrated groan.

'Don't worry,' Jack soothed. 'I'll keep my eyes shut, I promise.'

They should have all been exhausted. Even the patients who had stayed up to view what they could see of the fireworks from the verandahs hadn't had the opportunity to sleep late. The builders had arrived promptly at 6 a.m. and the enthusiastic hammering and bandsaw noises as they put the platform together precluded any further rest for the inpatients. Not that anybody was complaining.

Hospital staff began arriving by 7 a.m., including many of those who weren't on duty. They stood about, chatting and watching as the bank of cameras and lights were set up, bouquets of flowers rearranged and cleaners rushed about making last-minute preparations.

'It sounds like the United Nations,' Karen remarked. She watched her whiteboard being removed a little wistfully.

Kevin Farrow's eyes scanned the busy foyer and then locked anxiously on the staircase. 'I hope someone's watching Jim Cooper,' he muttered.

Amanda laughed. 'Don't fret, Kevin. Jim's daughter is coming in. She's going to stay with him.' She gave Kevin a very direct look. 'Just as long as you hold up your end of the bargain.'

'My lips are sealed,' Kevin assured her.

Jack had gone to have breakfast with Dorothy. They both looked up when Amanda entered the room. She stared at them. 'Do you know, you both have exactly the same smile?'

Dorothy nodded in a pleased fashion. 'When I get my other suitcase from the hotel storage I'll show you a photograph. Jack looks very like my oldest brother.'

'I'll look forward to that.' Amanda deposited the box she was carrying on the end of Dorothy's bed.

'What's in there, dear?'

'Curling wand, brushes and make-up supplies,' Amanda answered happily. 'I've come to get you ready for your international stardom.'

'Oh.' Dorothy's face creased worriedly. 'I'm really rather nervous about all this.'

'You'll be great.' Jack leaned over and kissed the soft old cheek gently. 'I'm going to be very proud of my grandmother.'

Dorothy's nerves seemed to be under good control by the time she walked slowly down the stairs aided by Amanda and was settled in the armchair which was almost swamped by the banks of flowers surrounding it. A microphone was clipped to the collar of her summery, blue, flowered dress and Amanda stroked a final curl into place, before easing herself back through the throng to stand beside Jack on the landing of the stairs. His hand found hers and their fingers interlaced tightly. Nobody knew who started it but a chorus of 'Happy Birthday' began quietly and then the volume grew as all the spectators joined in. Amanda had tears on her cheeks as it finally died to an expectant silence.

'How do you feel, Miss McFadden?' a journalist asked.

Dorothy took a slow, deep breath. 'I have now lived for one hundred years,' she said a little tremulously, 'and I can honestly say that this is the happiest day of my life.' She raised a lacy handkerchief shakily and dabbed at her eyes. Amanda bit her lip and hoped the mascara was as tearproof as it claimed.

'Is there anything you'd like to say, Miss McFadden?' a hopeful voice called into the silence that had fallen.

'Yes, there is.' Dorothy paused again and Amanda saw her hand grip the bunched handkerchief in her lap. Her voice, initially emotional and frail, gained strength as she spoke carefully.

'I have viewed my life as a tapestry,' she said. 'A picture in isolation. In recent years I have come to understand that a life in isolation has no real meaning. The meaning only comes through its connection to the pictures of others.'

Amanda's hand tingled as Jack squeezed it more tightly. She leaned her head against his shoulder.

'I came to Ashburton to look for such a connection,' Dorothy continued. 'And I found it.' Her voice caught and her words wobbled a little more. 'I have found my grandson. Now my picture isn't an isolated one and it matters less that it is nearly finished. I can see it simply as part of a much larger picture. It has given my life a meaning I didn't think I could ever find.'

The clapping was as spontaneous as the chorus of 'Happy Birthday'. The interview seemed to have ended until Kevin Farrow started creating a channel through the crowded foyer. He had someone with him and Amanda chuckled as she recognised the young mother whose baby she and Jack had delivered only hours before. A new level of excitement broke out and the media representatives forgot entirely to question the new angle of Dorothy's newly discovered grandson. They all watched as the newborn baby was taken and laid in Dorothy McFadden's arms. Symbols of the past, present and future. The perfect ending to the story that had captured everyone's imagination. Cameras rolled and light bulbs flashed as Dorothy smiled down at the infant.

Jack's ear was against Amanda's. 'She's going to look even happier when it's her great-grandchild she's holding.'

Amanda nodded and then sighed, a little worried that the emotional situation might be too much for the centenarian. It took nearly another hour before she and Jack could rescue Dorothy and take her upstairs to her room. Amanda helped her onto her bed and went to pull the curtains closed.

'Leave them open, dear.'

'But you must rest, Dorothy. You've still got a wedding to get through today.'

'I will, dear. But there's something I must do first.'

Jack was arranging a soft woollen rug over Dorothy's legs. 'Leave that, Jack. Would you get my handbag for me, please? It's in the bottom of my locker.'

It was an effort for her to unclip the old bag. 'I had someone fetch this from the hotel's safe-deposit box yesterday,' Dorothy explained. She removed a thick envelope. 'It's my wedding present for you both.'

'But we told you not to,' Amanda protested.

Dorothy just smiled. 'I told you about my first husband, Douglas, didn't I?'

Jack nodded.

'He ran quite a large organisation,' Dorothy informed them. 'It went by the name of Starbright International.'

Amanda gasped.

'It was a long time ago that we came here. He was interested in the Bay of Islands property but was also told about a possibility in the south island. Douglas wasn't keen but I was. He purchased the entire farm but the house was subdivided off with a few acres and a condition that gave him an option to purchase that part of the property should it ever become available. He did it for me, though I never explained why I wanted it so much other than that I had worked there.' Dorothy closed her eyes a little wearily and then reached for a glass of water that stood on her locker. She sipped it and looked at the two sets of eyes watching intently from either side of her bed.

'When the house was offered for sale ten years or so ago I made sure the owner would be allowed to stay there until he died. I was keeping his home safe for him, do you see? Just in case he *was* who I thought he was.' Dorothy's hand shook badly as she held out the envelope to Jack.

'Ashcroft is yours now, Jack. Yours and Amanda's. And the farm. It's been well managed as far as I can tell. The income should be enough to allow you to restore the house. It's where the Armstrongs belong.'

'And where you belong,' Jack added softly. 'Without you the Armstrongs would have vanished. I wouldn't be here.'

Dorothy closed her eyes more firmly. 'We're part of the same picture.' She nodded. 'I'm very proud of that.'

'You'd have to give up your nursing,' Jack warned. 'I don't want you to stop doing a job that you love so much.'

'I'll have to give up anyway if I'm going to organise the restoration of Ashcroft. That's a huge job. And if I keep working now then Jefferson is going to grow up into a total delinquent.' Amanda laughed suddenly—a wry chuckle.

'What's funny?'

'I got sick of the hype about this millennium change. I thought it was an interesting event but there was no way it was going to make the changes in people's lives that they seemed to expect. And look at me!'

'It might be too much of a change all at once.'

'No.' Amanda shook her head. 'I'm more than ready for it. Besides, I would love to nurse Dorothy. She's a special friend and she's going to need a lot of care from now on.'

'It's certainly what I would wish for myself,' Jack said quietly. 'To be cared for—at Ashcroft—by my own grandchildren.'

'You'll have to have children first,' Amanda smiled.

'Absolutely. And I think we'd better get on with it.' Jack reached for Amanda and she went willingly into his arms. 'We've still got an hour or two before we need to turn up to our wedding,' he murmured.

'Your place or mine?' Amanda whispered.

'Ours,' Jack replied firmly. 'Ashcroft.' His voice softened. 'Don't you think it's the best possible way to start a new millennium?'

'Oh, yes,' Amanda agreed fervently. *'Absolutely!'*

MILLS & BOON®

Makes
any time
special

Enjoy a romantic novel from
Mills & Boon®

Presents...™ *Enchanted*™ TEMPTATION.

Historical Romance™ ✓**MEDICAL**
ROMANCE™

MILLS & BOON®

MEDICAL ROMANCE™

VETS AT CROSS PURPOSES by Mary Bowring

Rose Deakin's job in David Langley's practice was hard because of her ex-fiancé, for David didn't employ couples. And he thought Rose still cared for Pete.

A MILLENNIUM MIRACLE by Josie Metcalfe
Bundles of Joy

Kara had a wonderful wedding present for Mac—she was pregnant! But her joy turned to fear when a car smash put Mac in a life-threatening coma…

A CHANGE OF HEART by Alison Roberts
Bachelor Doctors

Lisa Kennedy seemed immune to David James—how could he convince her that he would happily give up his bachelor ways for her?

HEAVEN SENT by Carol Wood

Locum Dr Matt Carrig evoked responses in widowed GP Dr Abbie Ashby she hadn't felt in a long time. Could she risk her heart, when Matt seemed intent on returning to Australia?

Available from 7th January 2000

MILLS & BOON®

MISTLETOE *Magic*

Three favourite Enchanted™ authors
bring you romance at Christmas.

Three stories in one volume:

A Christmas Romance
BETTY NEELS

Outback Christmas
MARGARET WAY

Sarah's First Christmas
REBECCA WINTERS

Published 19th November 1999

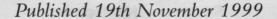

*Available at most branches of WH Smith, Tesco,
Martins, Borders, Easons, Volume One/James Thin
and most good paperback bookshops*

10...9...8...

As the clock struck midnight three single people became instant parents...

Millennium baby

Kristine Rolofson
Baby, It's Cold Outside

Bobby Hutchinson
One-Night-Stand Baby

Judith Arnold
Baby Jane Doe

Celebrate the Millennium with these three heart-warming stories of instant parenthood

Available from 24th December

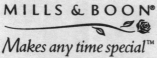

FREE
2 BOOKS
AND A SURPRISE GIFT!

We would like to take this opportunity to thank you for reading this Mills & Boon® book by offering you the chance to take TWO more specially selected titles from the Medical Romance™ series absolutely FREE! We're also making this offer to introduce you to the benefits of the Reader Service™—

    ★ FREE home delivery   ★ FREE gifts and competitions
    ★ FREE monthly Newsletter   ★ Exclusive Reader Service discounts
                ★ Books available before they're in the shops

Accepting these FREE books and gift places you under no obligation to buy; you may cancel at any time, even after receiving your free shipment. Simply complete your details below and return the entire page to the address below. *You don't even need a stamp!*

YES! Please send me 2 free Medical Romance books and a surprise gift. I understand that unless you hear from me, I will receive 4 superb new titles every month for just £2.40 each, postage and packing free. I am under no obligation to purchase any books and may cancel my subscription at any time. The free books and gift will be mine to keep in any case.

M9EC

Ms/Mrs/Miss/Mr ....Initials ....
BLOCK CAPITALS PLEASE

Surname ....

Address ....

....

....Postcode ....

Send this whole page to:
UK: FREEPOST CN81, Croydon, CR9 3WZ
EIRE: PO Box 4546, Kilcock, County Kildare (stamp required)

Offer valid in UK and Eire only and not available to current Reader Service subscribers to this series. We reserve the right to refuse an application and applicants must be aged 18 years or over. Only one application per household. Terms and prices subject to change without notice. Offer expires 30th June 2000. As a result of this application, you may receive further offers from Harlequin Mills & Boon Limited and other carefully selected companies. If you would prefer not to share in this opportunity please write to The Data Manager at the address above.

Mills & Boon is a registered trademark owned by Harlequin Mills & Boon Limited.
Medical Romance is being used as a trademark.